BOOKS BY KURT VONNEGUT, JR.

HAPPY BIRTHDAY, WANDA JUNE

A PLAY BY
KURT VONNEGUT, JR.

HAPPY BIRTHDAY, WANDA JUNE

DIAL PRESS TRADE PAPERBACKS

2020 Dial Press Trade Paperback Edition

Published in the United States by The Dial Press, an imprint of Random House,
a division of Penguin Random House LLC, New York.

THE DIAL PRESS is a registered trademark and the colophon is a trademark of Penguin
Random House LLC.

Originally published in hardcover and in slightly different form in the United States by
Delacorte Press/Seymour Lawrence, an imprint of Random House, a division of
Penguin Random House LLC, in 1970 and with additional material in 1971.

ISBN 978-0-385-28386-1
EBook ISBN 978-0-593-22941-5

Printed in the United States of America on acid-free paper

randomhousebooks.com

Cover design: Lynn Buckley

ABOUT THIS PLAY

This play is what I did when I was forty-seven years old—when my six children were children no more. It was a time of change, of good-bye and good-bye and good-bye. My big house was becoming a museum of vanished childhoods—of my vanished young manhood as well.

This was on Cape Cod. There were widows all around me—in houses like mine.

I was drinking more and arguing a lot, and I had to get out of that house.

I was supposedly a right-handed person, but I found myself using my left hand more and more. It became the hand that did most of the giving and taking for me. I asked my older brother what he knew about this. He said that I had been an ambidextrous infant. I had been taught to favor my right hand.

"I'm left-handed now, and I'm through with novels," I told him. "I'm writing a play. It's plays from now on."

I was writing myself a new family and a new early manhood. I was going to fool myself, and spooks in a novel couldn't do the job. I had to hire actors—pay them to say what I wished them to say, to dress as I wished them to dress, to laugh, to cry, to come or go when I said to.

Strictly speaking, I was rewriting an old play of mine. But that old play had been written by a right-handed stranger fifteen years my junior.

Fifteen years ago my wife and I conducted a Great Books program on Cape Cod. And when we read and discussed *The Odyssey,* the behavior of Odysseus at his homecoming struck me as cruelly preposterous. So I wrote a play about it, which I called *Penelope.*

Ernest Hemingway was still alive and seemingly well. So I felt free to imagine a modern Odysseus who was a lot like that part of Hemingway which I detested—the slayer of nearly extinct animals which meant him no harm.

The play was performed for one week at the Orleans Arena Theatre on the Cape. Harold Ryan, the hero, had a line in that version which went like this: "Things die. All things die." After the play closed at Orleans, I said that to my wife, and I returned to writing short stories and novels.

As a footnote to American theatrical history: the Orleans Arena Theatre, run by Gordon and Betsy Argo, produced six new plays by unknown writers, with no financial help from anyone.

During that same year, the Ford Foundation underwrote the production of ten new plays—at a cost of a hundred thousand dollars or more.

The Argos lost something like three hundred and nineteen dollars that year. So it goes.

. . .

Penelope, which became *Happy Birthday, Wanda June,* has been around so long that it was once optioned by Estelle Parsons—before she decided to be an actress. Think of that. Estelle used to suppose that she would be a producer some day.

She failed to produce *Penelope* for this reason: it was a lousy play. Actors complained that there were no parts for stars, that everybody got to talk as much as everybody else, that nobody changed or was proved right or wrong at the end.

This intolerable balancing of characters and arguments reflected my true feelings: I felt and I still feel that everybody is right, no matter what he says. I had, in fact, written a book about everybody's being right all the time, *The Sirens of Titan.* And I gave a name in that book to a mathematical point where all opinions, no matter how contradictory, harmonized. I called it a *chrono-synclastic infundibulum.*

I live in one.

Somewhere in there my father died, and one of the last things he said to me was that I had never written a story with a villain in it. That was surely one of the troubles with my play—and that remains a major trouble with it to this day. Even after we opened *Happy Birthday, Wanda June,* we experimented shamelessly with endings. We had various people shoot Harold, including children. We had Harold shoot various people, including children. We had Harold do the world the favor of shooting himself.

Nothing satisfied, and I am persuaded that nothing could satisfy, since the author did not have the balls to make Harold or anybody thoroughly vile.

. . .

That was chickenhearted of me. It was Edgar Lee Masters' *Spoon River Anthology,* and some other things, which has made me chickenhearted about villainy. I marveled at all the epitaphs in Masters' book when I was only twelve years old, and I was bound to say to myself, "My gosh—all those people *had* to be what they were."

My father and mother also tended to make me chickenhearted. My father was a frail architect and painter. He was also a gun nut, which used to amaze me. It seemed so inharmonious with the rest of him, that he should fondle guns.

He left me some guns.

My two siblings didn't like his gunplay, either. One time, I remember, my brother looked at a quail Father had shot, and he said, "My gosh—that's like smashing a fine Swiss watch." My sister used to cry and refuse to eat when Father brought home game.

Some homecoming for Odysseus!

Lester Goldsmith produced my play. He had never produced a play before. He used to be an executive at Paramount Pictures. And then he became an independent producer of political films. We met in the spring of 1970, at the home of Don Farber, who was a lawyer for both of us.

Lester remembered having read a synopsis of *Penelope,* which my agents had circulated around Hollywood years before. After we'd all had a few drinks, he said, "I'll option that play."

Which he did. And I went home and rewrote it all summer long.

Lester and I were inspired amateurs where legitimate theater was concerned. We remain good friends. God willing, we'll produce more plays less amateurishly.

Lester hired a theater before we had a script. And he moved so quickly that we needed a director almost immediately. No New York director was willing to take the job without a finished script in hand. What I had to show at that point, two months before opening night, was a filthy tossed salad of corrasable bond.

A television director from the West Coast examined the tossed salad. He was a good man who had directed such gruesome enterprises as *Gilligan's Island* and *The Art Linkletter Show*. He had done a lot of little theater, too, and had as his happiest memories the days when he had been the director of the road company of *Mr. Roberts*. His name was Michael J. Kane.

Mike and I must have come within a few hundred yards of each other in 1949 or so, when I saw his production of *Mr. Roberts* in Schenectady, New York. I was a public relations man at the time. That was where I learned my nice manners—as a public relations man.

I told Mike, when we met in New York City, that I had seen his show so long ago. We were nearly the same age, and he was so deep into remembering his youth that he said to me, without any hesitation, "Schenectady! My God how it snowed!"

He agreed to direct *Happy Birthday, Wanda June*. He was running away from home and some other things—for a little while. So was I. So was Lester.

* * *

It is my opinion that the writer and the producer and the director were pleasant, enthusiastic fools about theater. But Mike assembled a cast, headed by Kevin McCarthy, which was the equal of any cast in New York. Eliot Norton, the Boston critic, told me in conversation that our actors worked together as excitingly as Englishmen. High praise! I said of them, toward the end, "They're like The Harlem Globetrotters! Look at 'em go!"

The main trouble was with the author, who didn't really know what he was doing—except running away from home. There I was: all alone in a tiny penthouse borrowed from a friend, six doors down and fifteen floors up from the Theatre de Lys, where the actors were rehearsing. I was writing new beginnings and middles and ends. My nice manners and neat appearance decayed. I came to resemble a madman who was attempting to extract moonbeams from excrement.

We opened on October 7, 1970, at the de Lys. The reviews were mixed, as they say. We had actors, but no play—or, worse, we had an awfully long, old-fashioned play with no ending. We kept running, though.

And I kept rewriting. I became pathologically suggestible. If somebody had told me to paint my feet blue for the sake of the play, I would have done it solemnly. Blue-footed, I would have asked Lester to do what I was always asking him, "All right—we're ready. Invite Clive Barnes and John Simon to have another look." I would do anything anybody told me to do—but go home.

I now thank heaven that my main advisors were the actors, my new family. Their advice, particularly Kevin McCarthy's advice, was expert and beautiful. I was still rewriting six weeks after we opened. And along came an off-Broadway actors' strike.

So we tottered uptown to the Edison Theatre, and opened

again. We closed there on March 14, 1971, after 142 perfor-
mances. There was standing room only at the final perfor-
mance, a Sunday matinee. Some good soul shouted, "Bravo!"
The actors had saved the play.

Things die. All things die. My new family dissolved into
the late afternoon. As we went our separate ways out of the
theater district, blue movies and peepshows offered to con-
firm our new solitude, if we cared to drop in.

Walking home along Forty-seventh Street, I remembered
having asked Kevin and Nick Coster and Marsha Mason
what the end would be like. This was during supper at
Duff's, shortly after rehearsals had begun. "Does being in a
play with a person often make that person a friend for life?"
I said.

"You'd think it would—and I always think it will," said
Nick.

"When a play closes," said Marsha, "everybody promises
everybody else that they will go on seeing a lot of each other. . . ."
She paused to remember the closings she had endured.

Kevin finished the thought for her brusquely, unsenti-
mentally, in the manner of Ernest Hemingway. "But they
don't," he said. He took an iron-jawed bite of hot bread with
garlic butter. The subject was closed.

Here is who the members of my new family were—and I
list them in the order of their appearance in our posters and
ads:

KEVIN McCARTHY—Harold Ryan

KEITH CHARLES—Dr. Norbert Woodly

NICOLAS COSTER—Herb Shuttle

WILLIAM HICKEY—Col. Looseleaf Harper

MARSHA MASON—Penelope Ryan

LOUIS TURENNE—Siegfried von Konigswald

STEVEN PAUL—Paul Ryan

ARIANE MUNKER—Wanda June

ELLEN DANO—Wanda June (After Ariane became exhausted)

PAMELA SAUNDERS—Mildred Ryan

JESS OSUNA—Understudy for all the men

DIANE WIEST—Understudy for both women

Both understudies got on, and brought with them exciting new stuff.

ED WITTSTEIN—Settings

DAVID F. SEGAL—Lighting

JOSEPH G. AULISI—Costumes

GARY HARRIS—Sound

WALTER ROSEN SCHOLZ—Associate Producer

PAUL JOHN AUSTIN—Stage Manager

Auf wiedersehen!

HAPPY BIRTHDAY, WANDA JUNE

CAST

PENELOPE RYAN, 30

PAUL RYAN, 12, her son

HAROLD RYAN, 55, her husband

COLONEL LOOSELEAF HARPER, 50, her husband's
  sidekick

HERB SHUTTLE, 35, a suitor

DR. NORBERT WOODLY, 35, a suitor

WANDA JUNE, 10, a ghost

MAJOR SIEGFRIED VON KONIGSWALD, 50, a
  German ghost

MILDRED, 45, Harold's former wife, a ghost

ACT ONE

SCENE ONE

SILENCE. Pitch blackness. Animal eyes begin to glow in the darkness. Sounds of the jungle climax in animals fighting. A SINGER is heard singing the first bars of "All God's Chillun Got Shoes." HAROLD, LOOSELEAF, PENELOPE, and WOODLY stand in a row in the darkness, facing the audience. They are motionless. A city skyline in the early evening materializes outside the windows.

The lights come up on the living room of a rich man's apartment, which is densely furnished with trophies of hunts and wars. There is a front door, a door to the master bedroom suite, and a corridor leading to other bedrooms, the kitchen and so on.

PENELOPE

How do you do. My name is Penelope Ryan. This is a simple-minded play about men who enjoy killing—and those who don't.

HAROLD

I am Harold Ryan, her husband. I have killed perhaps two hundred men in wars of various sorts—as a professional soldier. I have killed thousands of other animals as well—for sport.

WOODLY

I am Dr. Norbert Woodly—a physician, a healer. I find it disgusting and frightening that a killer should still be a respected member of society. Gentleness must replace violence everywhere, or we are doomed.

PENELOPE

[To LOOSELEAF]

Would you like to say something about killing, Colonel?

LOOSELEAF

[Embarrassed]

Jesus—I dunno. You know. What the heck. Who knows?

PENELOPE

Colonel Harper, retired now, dropped an atom bomb on Nagasaki during the Second World War, killing seventy-four thousand people in a flash.

LOOSELEAF

I dunno, boy.

PENELOPE

You don't *know*?

LOOSELEAF

It was a bitch.

PENELOPE

Thank you.

[To all]

You can leave now. We'll begin.

WOODLY

[To the audience, making a peace sign]

Peace!

[All but PENELOPE exit]

PENELOPE

[To the audience]

This is a tragedy. When it's done, my face will be as white as the snows of Kilimanjaro.

[Hyena laughs]

My husband, who kills so much, has been missing for eight years. He disappeared in a light plane over the Amazon Rain Forest, where he hoped to find diamonds as big as cantaloupes. His pilot was Colonel Looseleaf Harper, who dropped the bomb on Nagasaki.

[Hyena laughs]

I should explain the doorbells in this apartment. They were built by Abercrombie and Fitch. They are actual recordings of animal cries. The back doorbell is a hyena, which you've just heard. The front doorbell is a lion's roar.

[To the wings]

Would you let them hear it please?

[Lion roars]

Thank you.

[PAUL, *her twelve-year-old son, enters from corridor, a sensitive, neatly dressed little rich boy*]

And this is my son, Paul. He was only four years old when his father disappeared.

PAUL
[*Radiantly, sappily*]

He's coming back, Mom! He's the bravest, most wonderful man who ever lived.

PENELOPE
[*To audience*]

I told you this was a simple-minded play.

PAUL

Maybe he'll come back tonight! It's his birthday.

PENELOPE

I know.

PAUL

Stay home tonight!

PENELOPE
[*Ruefully, for they have been over this before*]

Oh, Paul—

PAUL

You're married! You've already got a husband!

PENELOPE

He's a ghost!

PAUL

He's alive!

PENELOPE

Not even Mutual of Omaha thinks so anymore.

PAUL

If you have to go out with some guy—can't he be more
like Dad?

[Sick]

Herb Shuttle and Norbert Woodly—can't you do better
than those two freaks?

PENELOPE

[Resentfully]

Thank you, kind sir.

PAUL

A vacuum cleaner salesman and a fairy doctor.

PENELOPE

A what kind of doctor?

PAUL

A fairy—a queer. Everybody in the building knows he's a
queer.

PENELOPE

[Knowing better]

That's an interesting piece of news.

PAUL

You're the only woman he ever took out.

PENELOPE

Not true.

PAUL

Still lives with his mother.

PENELOPE

You know she has no *feet*! You want him to abandon his mother, who has no husband, who has no money of her own, who has no feet?

PAUL

How did she lose her feet?

PENELOPE

In a railroad accident many years ago.

PAUL

I was afraid to ask.

PENELOPE

Norbert was just beginning practice. A real man would have sold her to a catfood company, I suppose. As far as that goes, J. Edgar Hoover still lives with his mother.

PAUL

I didn't know that.

PENELOPE

A lot of people don't.

PAUL

J. Edgar Hoover plays sports.

PENELOPE

I don't really know.

PAUL

The only exercise Dr. Woodly ever gets is playing the violin and making that stupid peace sign.

[He makes the peace sign and says the word effeminately]

Peace. Peace. Peace, everybody.

[Lion doorbell roars]

PENELOPE

[Cringing]

I hate that thing.

PAUL

It's beautiful.

[He goes to door, admits WOODLY, *whom he loathes openly]*

WOODLY

[Wearing street clothes, carrying a rolled-up poster under his arm]

Peace, everybody—Paul, Penelope.

PAUL

You're taking Mom out tonight?

WOODLY

[To PENELOPE]

You're going out?

PENELOPE

Herb Shuttle is taking me to a fight.

WOODLY

Take plenty of cigars.

PENELOPE

[An apology, secret from PAUL]

We made the date three months ago.

WOODLY

I must take you to an emergency ward sometime—on a Saturday night. That's also fun. I came to see Selma, as a matter of fact.

PENELOPE

She quit this afternoon.

PAUL

We don't have a maid any more.

WOODLY

Oh?

PENELOPE

The animals made her sneeze and cry too much.

WOODLY

I'm glad somebody finally cried. Every time I come in here and see all this unnecessary death, *I* want to cry.

[Winking at PAUL, *acknowledging* PAUL's *low opinion of him]*

I don't cry, of course. Not manly, you know. Did she try antihistamines?

PENELOPE

They made her so sleepy she couldn't work.

WOODLY

Throw out all this junk. Burn it! This room crawls with tropical disease.

PAUL

Everything stays as it is!

WOODLY

A monument to a man who thought that what the world needed most was more rhinoceros meat.

PAUL

[Hotly]

My father!

WOODLY

I apologize. But you didn't know him, and neither did I. How's your asthma?

PAUL

Don't worry about it.

WOODLY

How's the fungus around your thumbnail?

PAUL

[Concealing the thumb]

It's fine!

WOODLY

It's jungle rot! This room is making everybody sick! This is your family doctor speaking now.

[Unrolling the poster]

Here—I brought you something else to hang on your wall, for the sake of variety.

PENELOPE

[Reading]

"War is not healthy for children and other living things." How lovely.

WOODLY

No doubt Paul thinks it stinks.

[Lion doorbell roars]

I hate that thing.

PAUL

[Going to the door]

Keeps fairies away!

[*He admits* HERB SHUTTLE, *who carries an Electrolux vacuum cleaner*]

SHUTTLE

[*To* PAUL *affectionately, touching him*]

Hi kid.

[*Seeing* WOODLY]

Would you look what the cat dragged in.

WOODLY

I'm glad you brought your vacuum cleaner.

SHUTTLE

Is that a fact?

WOODLY

The maid just quit. The place is a mess. You can start in the master bedroom.

PENELOPE

Please—

SHUTTLE

He's not anybody to tell somebody else what to do in a master bedroom.

PENELOPE

I'll get ready, Herb. I didn't expect you this soon.

[*To all*]

Please—won't everybody be nice to everybody else while I'm gone?

[*All freeze, except for* PENELOPE, *who comes forward to address the audience. Lights on set fade as spotlight comes on*]

Most men shunned me—even when I nearly swooned for want of love. I might as well have been girdled in a chastity belt. My chastity belt was not made of iron and chains and chickenwire, but of Harold's lethal reputation.

[SHUTTLE *comes into the spotlight*]

SHUTTLE

I keep having this nightmare—that he catches us.

PENELOPE

Doing what?

SHUTTLE

He'd kill me. He'd be right to kill me, too—the kind of guy he is.

PENELOPE

Or was. We haven't done anything wrong, you know.

SHUTTLE

He'd assume we had.

PENELOPE

That's something, I suppose.

SHUTTLE

All through the day I'm so confident. That's why I'm such a good salesman, you know? I have confidence, and I look like I have confidence, and that gives other people confidence. People laugh sometimes when they find out I'm a vacuum cleaner salesman. They stop laughing, though, when they find out I made forty-three thousand dollars last year. I've got six other salesmen working under me, and what they all plug into is *my* confidence. That's what charges them up.

PENELOPE

I'm glad.

SHUTTLE

I was captain of the wrestling team at Lehigh University.

PENELOPE

I know.

SHUTTLE

If you want to wrestle, you go to Lehigh. If you want to play tennis, you go to Vanderbilt.

PENELOPE

I don't want to go to Vanderbilt.

SHUTTLE

You don't wrestle if you don't have supreme confidence, and I wrestled. But when I get with you, and I say to myself, "My God—here I am with the wife of Harold Ryan, one of the great heroes of all time—"

[Pause]

PENELOPE

Yes?

SHUTTLE

Something happens to my confidence.

PENELOPE

[To the audience]

This conversation took place, incidentally, about three months before Harold was declared legally dead.

SHUTTLE

When Harold is definitely out of the picture, Penelope, when I don't have to worry about doing him wrong or you wrong or Paul wrong, I'm going to ask you to be my wife.

PENELOPE

I'm touched.

SHUTTLE

That's when I'll get my confidence back.

PENELOPE

I see.

SHUTTLE

If you'll pardon the expression, that's when you'll see the fur and feathers fly. Good night.

PENELOPE

Good night.

[Blackout]

SCENE TWO

SHUTTLE and WOODLY argue in pitch darkness, with PAUL listening, and lights come up gradually to full on the living room the same evening.

SHUTTLE

You've got to fight from time to time.

WOODLY

Not true.

SHUTTLE

Or get eaten alive.

WOODLY

That's not true either—or needn't be, unless we make it true.

SHUTTLE

Phooey.

WOODLY

Which we do. But we can stop doing that.

[The lights are full. SHUTTLE and WOODLY are bored with each other. WOODLY looks out the window, speaks to an imaginary listener who has more brains than SHUTTLE. PAUL hates them both, but prefers SHUTTLE's noisy manliness]

We simply stop doing that—dropping things on each other, eating each other alive.

SHUTTLE

[Calling]

Penelope! We're late!

PENELOPE

[Off, in master bedroom suite]

Coming.

SHUTTLE

[To PAUL]

Women are always late. You'll find out.

WOODLY

[Thoughtfully]

The late Mrs. Harold Ryan.

SHUTTLE

I'm sick of this argument. I just have one more thing to say: If you elect a President, you support him, no matter what he does. That's the only way you can have a country!

WOODLY

It's the planet that's in ghastly trouble now and all our brothers and sisters thereon.

SHUTTLE

None of my relatives are Chinese Communists. Speak for yourself.

WOODLY

Chinese maniacs and Russian maniacs and American maniacs and French maniacs and British maniacs have turned this lovely, moist, nourishing blue-green ball into a doomsday device. Let a radar set and a computer mistake a hawk or a meteor for a missile, and that's the end of mankind.

SHUTTLE

You can believe that if you want. I talk to guys like you, and I want to commit suicide.

[To PAUL]

You get that weight-lifting set I sent you?

PAUL

It came yesterday. I haven't opened it yet.

WOODLY

[Musingly, attempting to find the idea acceptable, even funny, in a way]

Maybe it's supposed to end now. Maybe God wouldn't have it any other way.

SHUTTLE

[To PAUL]

Start with the smallest weights. Every week add a pound or two.

WOODLY

Maybe God has let everybody who ever lived be reborn—
so he or she can see how it ends. Even Pithecanthropus
erectus and Australopithecus and Sinanthropus pekensis
and the Neanderthalers are back on Earth—to see how it
ends. They're all on Times Square—making change for
peepshows. Or recruiting Marines.

SHUTTLE

[To PAUL]

You ever hear the story about the boy who carried a calf
around the barn every day?

WOODLY

He died of a massive rupture.

SHUTTLE

You think you're so funny. You're not even funny.

[To PAUL]

Right? Right? You don't hurt yourself if you start out
slow.

WOODLY

You're preparing him for a career in the slaughterhouses of
Dubuque?

[To PAUL]

Take care of your body, yes! But don't become a bender of
horseshoes and railroad spikes. Don't become obsessed by
your musculature. Any one of these poor, dead animals

here was a thousand times the athlete you can ever hope to be. Their magic was in their muscles. Your magic is in your brains!

[PENELOPE *enters from the bedroom, dressed for the fight. She wears barbaric jewelry* HAROLD *gave her years ago, a jaguar-skin coat over her shoulders*]

PENELOPE

[*Brightly*]

Gentlemen! Is this right for a fight? It's been so long.

SHUTTLE

Beautiful! I've never seen that coat.

PENELOPE

Seven jaguars' skins, I'm told. Harold shot every one. Shall we go?

WOODLY

[*Sick about the slain jaguars*]

Oh no! Wear a coat of cotton—wear a coat of wool.

PENELOPE

What?

WOODLY

Wear a coat of domestic mink. For the love of God, though, Penelope, don't lightheartedly advertise that the last of the jaguars died for you.

SHUTTLE

She's my date tonight. What do you want her to do—
bring the poor old jaguars back to life with a bicycle
pump? Bugger off! Ask Paul what *he* thinks.

[*To* PAUL]

Your mother looks beautiful—right?

[PAUL *pointedly declines to answer*]

Kid?

[PAUL *walks away from him*]

Doesn't your mother look nice?

[*He goes to* PAUL, *wondering what is wrong*]

Paul?

PAUL

[*Smolderingly*]

I don't care what she wears.

SHUTTLE

Something's made you sore.

PAUL

Don't worry about it.

SHUTTLE

You bet I'll worry about it. I said something wrong?

PAUL

[*Close to angry tears*]

It's my father's birthday—that's all.

[Facing everybody, raising his voice]

That's all. Who cares about that?

SHUTTLE

[Horrified, raising his hand to swear an oath]

I had not the slightest inkling.

[To PENELOPE, feeling betrayed]

Why didn't you say so?

PAUL

[Bitterly]

She doesn't care! She's not married any more! She's going to have fun!

[To PENELOPE]

I hope you have so much fun you can hardly stand it.

[To WOODLY]

Dr. Woodly—I hope you make up even better jokes about my father than the ones you've said so far.

SHUTTLE

[Reaching out for PAUL]

Kid—kid—

PAUL

[To SHUTTLE]

And I wish you'd quit touching me all the time. It drives
me nuts!

SHUTTLE

[Reaching out again]

What's this?

PAUL

[Recoiling]

Don't!

SHUTTLE

[Aghast]

You sure misunderstood something—and we'd better get it
straight.

PAUL

Explain it to them. I'm bugging out of here.

[He grabs a jacket from a chair. SHUTTLE is in his way]

Don't touch me. Get out of the way.

SHUTTLE

Men can touch other men, and it doesn't mean a thing.
Haven't you ever seen football players after they've won the
Superbowl?

PENELOPE

[To PAUL]

Where will you be?

PAUL

Anywhere but here. I'd just sit here and cry about the way
my father's been forgotten.

SHUTTLE

I *worship* your father. That stuffed alligator your mother
gave me—the one he shot? It's the proudest thing in my
apartment.

PAUL

[At the door]

Everybody talks about how rotten kids act. Grownups can
be pretty rotten, too.

[He exits through front door, slams it]

SHUTTLE

[Heartbroken]

Kid—kid—

WOODLY

It's good. Let him go.

SHUTTLE

If he'd just come out for the Little League, the way I asked
him, he'd find out we touch all the time—shove each
other, slug each other, and just horse around. I'm going to
go get him—

WOODLY

Don't! Let him have all the privacy he wants. Let him grieve,
let him rage. There has never been a funeral for his father.

PENELOPE

I never knew when to hold it—or who to ask, or what to say.

WOODLY

Tonight's the night.

SHUTTLE

If he'd just get into scouting, and camp out some, and see how everybody roughhouses around the fire—

WOODLY

What a beautiful demonstration this is of the utter necessity of rites of passage.

SHUTTLE

I feel like I've been double-crossed.

[To PENELOPE, peevishly]

If you'd just told me it was Harold's birthday—

PENELOPE

What then?

SHUTTLE

We could have had some kind of birthday party for him. We could have taken Paul to the fight with us.

WOODLY

Minors aren't allowed at fights.

SHUTTLE

Then we'd stay home and eat venison or something,
and look through the scrapbooks. I've got a friend
who has a whole freezer full of striped bass and caribou
meat.

[Going to the front door]

I'm going to bring that boy back.

[He exits through front door]

WOODLY

[Going to PENELOPE]

This is very good for us.

PENELOPE

It is?

WOODLY

The wilder Paul is tonight, the calmer he'll be tomorrow.

PENELOPE

As long as he keeps out of the park.

WOODLY

After this explosion, I think, he'll be able to accept the fact
that his mother is going to marry again.

PENELOPE

The only thing I ever told him about life was, "Keep out
of the park after the sun goes down."

WOODLY

We've got to dump Shuttle.

[Pointing to the vacuum cleaner]

He brings his vacuum cleaner on *dates*?

PENELOPE

That's the XKE.

WOODLY

The what?

PENELOPE

It's an experimental model. He doesn't dare leave it in his car, for fear it will fall into the hands of competition.

WOODLY

What kind of a life is that?

PENELOPE

He told me one time what the proudest moment of his life was. He made Eagle Scout when he was twenty-nine years old.

[Clinging to him suddenly]

Oh, Norbert—promise me that Paul has not gone into the park!

WOODLY

[Pause]

If you warned him against it as much as you say, it's almost a certainty.

PENELOPE

[Petrified]

No! Oh no! Three people murdered in there in the last six weeks! The police won't even go in there any more.

WOODLY

I wish Paul luck.

PENELOPE

It's suicide!

WOODLY

I'd be dead by now if that were the case.

PENELOPE

Meaning?

WOODLY

Every night, Penelope, for the past two years, I've made it a point to walk through the park at midnight.

PENELOPE

Why would you do that?

WOODLY

To show myself how brave I am. The issue's in doubt, you know—since I'm always for peace—

PENELOPE

I'm amazed.

WOODLY

Me, too. I know something not even the police know—
what's in the park at midnight. Nothing. Or, when I'm in
there, there's me in there. Fear and nobody and me.

PENELOPE

And maybe Paul. What about the murderers? They're in
there!

WOODLY

They didn't murder me.

PENELOPE

Paul's only twelve years old.

WOODLY

He can make the sound of human footsteps—which is a
terrifying sound.

PENELOPE

We've got to rescue him.

WOODLY

If he is in the park, luck is all that can save him now, and
there's plenty of that.

PENELOPE

He's not your son.

WOODLY

No. But he's going to be. If he is in the park and he comes
out safely on the other side, I can say to him, "You and I

are the only men with balls enough to walk through the park at midnight."

[Pause]

On that we can build.

    PENELOPE

It's a jungle out there.

    WOODLY

That's been said before.

    PENELOPE

He'd go to a movie. I think that's what he'd do. If I were sure he was in a movie, I could stop worrying. We could have him paged.

[Lion doorbell roars]

    WOODLY

I hate that thing.

[He opens door, admits SHUTTLE, who carries a bakery box]

    PENELOPE

Did you see him?

    SHUTTLE

Yeah.

    PENELOPE

Is he all right?

SHUTTLE

Far as I know.

PENELOPE

Is he coming home?

SHUTTLE

He ditched me. He started running, and I started running, then he lost me in the park.

PENELOPE

The park!

SHUTTLE

It's dark in there.

PENELOPE

And that's where he is!

SHUTTLE

I figure he ducked in one place and ducked out another.

PENELOPE

[Disgusted with him]

You figure!

SHUTTLE

Then I saw this bakery store that was still open, so I bought a birthday cake.

PENELOPE

A what?

SHUTTLE

For Harold. When Paul comes home, we can have some birthday cake.

PENELOPE

How nice.

SHUTTLE

They had this cake somebody else hadn't picked up. It says, "Happy Birthday, Somebody Else."

WOODLY

"Happy Birthday, Wanda June!"

SHUTTLE

We can take off the "Wanda June" with a butter knife.

PENELOPE

Did you talk to Paul?

SHUTTLE

Before he started to run. He said his father carried a key to this apartment around his neck—and someday we'd all hear the sound of that key in the door.

PENELOPE

We've got to find him.

[Preparing to exit through front door]

I want you to show me exactly where you saw him last.

[To WOODLY]

And you stay here, Norbert, in case he comes home.

[To SHUTTLE*]*

That's all he said—the thing about the key?

SHUTTLE

He said one other thing. It wasn't very nice.

PENELOPE

What was it?

SHUTTLE

He told me to take a flying fuck at the moon.

[Blackout]

SCENE THREE

DARKNESS. Lights come up on living room. WOODLY is alone, asleep on the couch.

HAROLD lets himself and LOOSELEAF in through the front door—quietly. HAROLD has a full beard and a paunch. LOOSELEAF is skinnier. He has a handlebar moustache. Both wear new sports clothes and smoke expensive cigars. HAROLD is calm. LOOSELEAF is nervous, confused. They prowl the room cautiously, checking this and that. HAROLD awakens WOODLY by playing with his feet.

    WOODLY
[Startled]

Ooops.

    HAROLD
[To LOOSELEAF, very amused]

Ooops.

    WOODLY
Can I—uh—help you gentlemen?

HAROLD

[Moving downstage, feeling at home]

Gentlemen—that's nice.

WOODLY

[To LOOSELEAF]

You startled me.

LOOSELEAF

Yeah. We just got here.

WOODLY

I thought you might be burglars—but you're not, I hope.

LOOSELEAF

Nope.

[Idiotically, incapable of deception]

I got a lot of stuff.

WOODLY

[Looking at him closely]

You do?

HAROLD

The door was unlocked. Is it always unlocked?

WOODLY

It's always *locked*.

HAROLD

But here *you* are inside, aren't you?

WOODLY

You're—you're old friends of Harold Ryan?

HAROLD

We tried to be. We tried to be.

WOODLY

He's dead, you know.

HAROLD

Dead! Such a *final* word. Dead!

[*To* LOOSELEAF]

Did you hear that?

LOOSELEAF

Yup.

[*Telephone rings.* WOODLY *answers, keeping his eyes on the bizarre guests*]

WOODLY

Hello? Oh—hello, Mother.

HAROLD

[*To* LOOSELEAF]

Hello, Mother.

WOODLY

. . . Who? . . . Did she say how far apart the pains were? . . . When was that? . . . Oh dear.

HAROLD

Oh dear.

WOODLY

Call her back—tell her to head for the hospital. Tell the hospital to expect her. I'll leave right now.

[He hangs up, faces the intruders]

Look—I'm sorry—I have to go.

HAROLD

We'll miss you so.

WOODLY

Look—this isn't my apartment, and there isn't anybody else here. Mrs. Ryan won't be home for a while.

HAROLD

Oh, oh, oh—I thought it *was* your apartment. You seemed so at home here.

WOODLY

I'm a neighbor. I have the apartment across the hall. I have to go to the hospital now. An *emergency*.

[HAROLD is unstirred]

I mean—I can't leave you here. You'll have to go. I'll tell Mrs. Ryan you were here. You can come back later.

HAROLD

Ahh—then she's still alive.

WOODLY

She's fine. Please—

HAROLD

And still Mrs. Harold Ryan?

WOODLY

Will you please go? An emergency!

HAROLD

She still has just the one child—the boy?

[He moves slowly toward the front door, with WOODLY trying to hustle him and LOOSELEAF out]

WOODLY

Yes! Yes! The boy! One boy!

HAROLD

[Stopping]

And what, exactly, is your relationship to Mrs. Ryan?

WOODLY

Neighbor! Doctor! I live across the hall.

HAROLD

And you come into Mrs. Ryan's apartment as often as you please, looking into various health matters?

WOODLY

Yes! Please! You've got to get out right now!

[HAROLD moves a little more, stops again]

HAROLD

Just her neighbor and doctor? That's all?

WOODLY

[At the end of his patience, blurting]

And her fiancé!

HAROLD

[Delighted]

And her fiancé! How nice. I hope you'll be very
happy—or is that what one says to the woman?

WOODLY

I've got to run!

[He turns out the overhead light]

HAROLD

You wish the woman good luck, and you tell the man how
fortunate he is. That's how it goes.

WOODLY

[Holding open the front door]

I've literally got to run!

HAROLD

I won't try to keep up with you. I'm not as fast on my feet
as I once was.

*[All three exit. A moment later, HAROLD lets himself and
LOOSELEAF in again with a key. He turns on the light again,
roams the room, reacquainting himself with his beloved trophies.
LOOSELEAF is jangled by the adventure. HAROLD chucks a lioness
under her chin]*

Miss me, baby?

LOOSELEAF

I dunno, boy.

HAROLD

Hm?

LOOSELEAF

It's a bitch.

HAROLD

[Quietly]

A bitch.

LOOSELEAF

Didn't recognize you.

HAROLD

We've never met.

LOOSELEAF

I wonder who'll recognize us first? They'll wet their pants.

HAROLD

I hope the men do. I would rather the women didn't.

LOOSELEAF

I'm gonna wet *my* pants.

[He laughs idiotically]

HAROLD

[Looking around himself]

Home, sweet home.

LOOSELEAF

One thing, anyway—at least Penelope didn't throw out all your crap. I bet Alice threw out all my crap after I'd been gone a week.

HAROLD

We'll see.

[HAROLD, who wants to savor the early moments of his homecoming alone, now tries to get the very jumpy LOOSELEAF out of the apartment]

It appears that we're going to have to wait awhile for any more action here, Colonel. Why don't you run on home while the evening's young.

LOOSELEAF

Home. Jesus.

[He makes his hands tremble]

I'm like *this.* Home!

HAROLD

Home is important to a man.

LOOSELEAF

You know what gets me?

HAROLD

[Absently]

No.

LOOSELEAF

How all the magazines show tits today.

HAROLD

Um.

LOOSELEAF

Used to be against the law, didn't it?

HAROLD

[Fed up with LOOSELEAF]

I suppose.

LOOSELEAF

[Making no move to leave]

Must have changed the law.

[Silence, while HAROLD attempts to be alone, even though LOOSELEAF is still present]

HAROLD

[Thoughtfully hefting a broadsword, admiring its balance and strength]

Home.

LOOSELEAF

You know what gets me?

[HAROLD does not respond]

You know what gets me?

HAROLD

[To himself]

Oh, shit.

LOOSELEAF

[Finding enough encouragement in this]

How everybody says "fuck" and "shit" all the time. I used to be scared shitless I'd say "fuck" or "shit" in public, by accident. Now everybody says "fuck" and "shit," "fuck" and "shit" all the time. Something very big must have happened while we were out of the country.

HAROLD

[Flatly]

Looseleaf—will you get the hell home?

LOOSELEAF

At least we found the diamonds.

HAROLD

At least!

LOOSELEAF

I'd really feel stupid if we didn't bring anything back home.

HAROLD

It's enough that you've brought yourself home!

LOOSELEAF

I wish you'd tell Alice that. And that Goddamn Mrs. Wheeler.

HAROLD

[Hotly]

Tell them yourself!

LOOSELEAF

You don't know my mother-in-law, boy.

HAROLD

After eight years in the jungle with you, I know Mrs.
Wheeler better than I know anybody in the universe!

LOOSELEAF

I didn't tell you everything.

HAROLD

The time we were in a tree for fourteen days, you certainly
tried to tell me everything about Mrs. Wheeler.

LOOSELEAF

I didn't even scratch the surface. You're lucky, boy. You
come home, and nobody's here. When I go home, *everybody's* going to be there.

HAROLD

This room is full of ghosts.

LOOSELEAF

You're lucky, boy. My house is gonna be filled with *people.*

[HAROLD *ignores this, attempts to savor the ghosts in the room*]

You know what gets me?

HAROLD

Go home!

LOOSELEAF

Thank God we found the fucking diamonds!

HAROLD

The hell with the diamonds!

LOOSELEAF

You were rich *before*. This is the first time I was ever rich.

HAROLD

Go home! Show them how rich you are for a change!

LOOSELEAF

Can I have the Cadillac?

HAROLD

Take the Cadillac and drive it off a cliff, for all I care.

LOOSELEAF

What'll you do for transportation?

HAROLD

I'll buy a hundred more Cadillacs. Go home!

LOOSELEAF

You know what gets me about that Cadillac?

HAROLD

Go home!

LOOSELEAF

When I drive it, I feel like I'm in the middle of a great big wad of bubblegum. I don't hear anything, I don't feel anything. I figure somebody else is driving. It's a bitch.

HAROLD

Go home.

LOOSELEAF

I'm liable to find anything!

HAROLD

That's the point! Walk in there and find whatever there *is* to find—before Alice can cover it up.

LOOSELEAF

I know, I know. I dunno. At least she's in the same house. Sure was spooky, looking in the window there, and there she was.

HAROLD

So long, Colonel.

LOOSELEAF

You know what gets me?

HAROLD

[Taking hold of LOOSELEAF *and steering him to the front door]*

Let's talk about it some other time.

LOOSELEAF

How short the skirts are.

HAROLD

[Opening the door]

Good night, Colonel. It's been beautiful.

LOOSELEAF

Something very important about sex must have happened while we were gone.

[HAROLD *shoves him out of the apartment and shuts the door.* HAROLD *starts to roam the room again, but the lion doorbell roars*]

HAROLD

[*Going to the door*]

Hell!

[HAROLD *opens the door.* LOOSELEAF *comes in*]

LOOSELEAF

You know what gets me? Those guys who went to the moon! To the *moon,* boy!

HAROLD

Leave me alone! After eight years of horrendously close association, the time has come to part! I crave solitude and time for reflection—and then a reunion in privacy with my own flesh and blood. You and I may not meet again for months!

LOOSELEAF

Months?

HAROLD

I'm certainly not going to come horning back into your life tomorrow, and I will not welcome your horning back into mine. A chapter has ended. We are old comrades—at a parting of the ways.

LOOSELEAF

[Bleakly, shrugging]

I'm lonesome already.

[He exits]

HAROLD

[Roaming the room again]

The moon. The new heroism—put a village idiot into a pressure cooker, seal it up tight, and shoot him at the moon.

[To his portrait]

Hello there, young man. In case you're wondering, I could beat the shit out of you. And any woman choosing between us—sorry, kid, she'd choose me.

[Pleased with the room]

I must say, this room is very much as I left it.

[He sees the cake]

What's this? A cake? "Happy Birthday, Wanda June"? Who the hell is Wanda June?

[Blackout]

SCENE FOUR

Music indicates happiness, innocence, and weightlessness. Spotlight comes up on WANDA JUNE, a lisping eight-year-old in a starched party dress. She is as cute as Shirley Temple.

WANDA JUNE

Hello. I am Wanda June. Today was going to be my birthday, but I was hit by an ice-cream truck before I could have my party. I am dead now. I am in Heaven. That is why my parents did not pick up the cake at the bakery. I am not mad at the ice-cream truck driver, even though he was drunk when he hit me. It didn't hurt much. It wasn't even as bad as the sting of a bumblebee. I am really *happy* here! It's so much fun. I am glad the driver was drunk. If he hadn't been, I might not have got to Heaven for years and years and years. I would have had to go to high school first, and then beauty college. I would have had to get married and have babies and everything. Now I can just play and play and play. Any time I want any pink cotton candy I can have some. Everybody up here is happy—the animals and the dead soldiers and people who went to the electric chair and everything. They're all glad for whatever sent them here. Nobody is mad. We're all too busy playing shuffleboard. So if you think of killing somebody, don't worry about it. Just go ahead and do it. Whoever you do it to should kiss you for doing it. The soldiers up here just love the shrapnel and the tanks and the bayonets and the dum dums that let them play shuffleboard all the time—and drink beer.

[Spotlight begins to dim and carnival music on a steam calliope begins to intrude, until, at the end of the speech, WANDA JUNE *is drowned out and the stage is black]*

We have merry-go-rounds that don't cost anything to ride on. We have Ferris wheels. We have Little League and girls' basketball. There's a drum and bugle corps anybody can join. For people who like golf, there is a par-three golf course and a driving range, with never any waiting. If you just want to sit and loaf, why that's all right, too. Gourmet specialties are cooked to your order and served at any time of night or day. . . .

[Sudden silence]

WOODY WOODPECKER VOICE

Ha ha ha *ha* ha!

[Pistol shot]

You got me, pal.

[Silence

Spotlight comes up on LOOSELEAF HARPER, *who wears the clothes he will wear in the next scene—new sports clothes, a shirt open at the neck. As always, he is friendly and embarrassed]*

LOOSELEAF

When Penelope asked me to say something about drop-ping the bomb on Nagasaki, I didn't give a very good answer, I guess. It's a very complicated question. Jesus—you *know*? You have to explain what it's like to be in the Air Force and how they give you your orders and all that. What it feels like to be in a plane, what the world looks like down there. After I got home from the war, the minister of my church asked me if I would speak to a scout troop that met in the church basement. So I did. They met on Thursday nights. I used to belong to that troop. I never made Eagle Scout. But you know some-thing? It's a very strange kind of kid that makes Eagle Scout. They always seem so lonesome, like they'd worked real hard to get a job nobody else cares about. They get a whole bunch of merit badges. That's how you get to be an Eagle Scout. I don't think I had over five or six merit badges. The only one I remember is Public Health. That was a bitch. The Boy Scout Manual said I was supposed to find out what my town did about sewage. Jesus, they just dumped it all in Sugar Creek.

[He laughs idiotically]

Sugar Creek! That was a long time ago, but it's all coming back to me now. There was another merit badge you could get for roller-skating. There used to be a roller rink at a bend in Sugar Creek, up above where the sewage went in. I got in a fight there one time. I had on roller skates, and the guy I was fighting had on basketball shoes. He had a tremendous advantage over me. He was a little guy, but he beat the shit out of me. I had to laugh like hell. Don't ever fight a guy when you've got on roller skates.

[Silence]

Jesus—I remember my mother used to make me chew bananas for a full minute before I swallowed—so I wouldn't get sick. Makes you wonder what else your parents told you that wasn't *true*.

[Blackout]

SCENE FIVE

Spotlight comes up on HAROLD. *He sits on the front seat of an imaginary car. The seat is covered with zebra skin.*

HAROLD

The night I met Penelope, I had no beard—so imagine me, if you can, without a beard. Actually, I wasn't as good-looking then as I am now. And, if anything, my health has improved. At any rate—I had just come home from Kenya—to discover that my third wife, Mildred, like the two before her, had become a drunken bum. In my experience, alcoholism is far more prevalent among women than men. So I got into my automobile—

[He pantomimes turning the ignition key. The sound of a starter and a powerful engine responds. He pantomimes putting the car in gear and driving away from the curb. Appropriate sounds are heard]

I drove through the night, until I was attracted by a sign which said—

[Spotlight comes up on PENELOPE, *who wears a skimpy carhop outfit she has had on under her coat]*

"Hamburger Heaven."

PENELOPE

Heaven.

[HAROLD *pantomimes swerving into Hamburger Heaven. Tires squeal. He pantomimes a stop, kills the engine. He blows his imaginary horn. A real horn blows the bugle call for "charge."* PENELOPE *crosses to* HAROLD]

Can I help you, sir?

HAROLD

I think so, daughter. How old are you?

PENELOPE

Eighteen—

[Pause]

and a half.

HAROLD

A springbok, an oryx, a gemsbok—a gazelle.

PENELOPE

Sir?

HAROLD

Raw hamburger, please—and a whole onion. I want to eat the onion like an apple. Do you understand?

PENELOPE

Yes, sir.

[To the audience]

It was a very unusual automobile. It was a Cadillac, but it had water buffalo horns where the bumpers should be.

[To HAROLD]

And what to drink?

HAROLD

What time do you get off work, my child?

PENELOPE

I'm sorry, sir, I'm engaged to be married. My boyfriend would be mad if I went out with another man.

HAROLD

Did you ever daydream that you would one day meet a friendly millionaire?

PENELOPE

I'm engaged.

HAROLD

Daughter—I love you very much.

PENELOPE

You don't even *know* me.

HAROLD

You are woman. I know woman well.

PENELOPE

This is crazy.

HAROLD

Destiny often seems that way. You're going to marry me.

PENELOPE

What do you do for a living?

HAROLD

My parents died in an automobile accident when I was sixteen years old. They left me a brewery and a baseball team—and other things. I *live* for a living. I've just come back from Kenya—in Africa. I've been hunting Mau Mau there.

PENELOPE

Some kind of animal?

HAROLD

The pelt is black. It's a kind of man.

[Blackout]

SCENE SIX

CURTAIN rises on empty living room. PAUL lets himself in with a key.

      PAUL

Mom?

[Silence]

Herb?

[Silence]

Dr. Woodly?

[He advances into room uneasily]

Hello?

[He sees the cake]

A cake? Who's Wanda June?

[HAROLD enters quietly from the kitchen, holding a can of beer]

Anybody home?

HAROLD

As a matter of fact—

PAUL

[Nearly jumping out of his skin]

Sir?

HAROLD

As a matter of fact—*I* am home.

PAUL

[Thinking HAROLD may be a burglar]

Hello.

HAROLD

[Simply]

Hello.

PAUL

Are you—

[His voice fails him]

HAROLD

[Hoping to be recognized]

You were about to ask a question?

PAUL

Are you—do you—

HAROLD

Ask it!

PAUL

[Blurting]

Do you know who Wanda June is?

HAROLD

Life has denied me that thrill.

PAUL

Do you mind if I ask who you are?

HAROLD

Mind?

[Aside]

God, yes, I mind.

[To PAUL*]*

I'm your father's friend. A man claiming to be the family physician let me in a while ago.

PAUL

Dr. Woodly.

HAROLD

Dr. Woodly. I should make a little list.

PAUL

Is anybody besides you here now?

HAROLD

The doctor was called away on an emergency. I think it was birth.

PAUL

Where's Mom?

HAROLD

You don't *know* where your mother is? Does she put on a short skirt and go drinking all night?

PAUL

She went to the fight with Herb Shuttle, I guess.

HAROLD

You think you could find me a pencil and paper?

PAUL

I'll see.

[He rummages through a drawer]

HAROLD

And you've been roaming the streets while your mother is God-knows-where?

PAUL

I was going to a funny movie, but I changed my mind. If you're depressed, laughing doesn't help much.

[He gives HAROLD pencil and paper]

When did you know my father?

HAROLD

Man and boy.

PAUL

Everybody says he was so brave.

HAROLD

Even this—"Herb Shuttle," you said?

PAUL

He *worships* Father.

HAROLD

[Pleased]

Ah! And what sort of man *is* this worshiper?

PAUL

He's a vacuum cleaner salesman.

HAROLD

[Deflated]

I see.

[Recovering]

And he came into the apartment one day, to demonstrate his wares, and your mother, as it happened, was charmingly *en deshabille*—

PAUL

She met him at college.

HAROLD

[Startled]

College!

PAUL

They were in the same creative writing class.

HAROLD

College?

PAUL

She has a master's degree in English literature.

HAROLD

What a pity! Educating a beautiful woman is like pouring honey into a fine Swiss watch. Everything stops.

[Pause]

And the doctor? He worships your father, too?

PAUL

He insults him all the time.

HAROLD

[Delighted]

Excellent!

PAUL

What's good about that?

HAROLD

It makes life spicy.

PAUL

He doesn't do it in front of me, but he does it with Mother.

[Indicating HAROLD's portrait]

You know what he called Father one time?

HAROLD

No.

PAUL

"Harold, the Patron Saint of Taxidermy."

HAROLD

[Measuring his opponent]

What does he do—of an athletic nature?

PAUL

Nothing. He plays a violin in a doctors' quartet.

HAROLD

Aha! He has a brilliant military record, I'm sure.

PAUL

He was a stretcher-bearer in the Korean War.

[Pause]

Were you in a war with Father?

HAROLD

Big ones, little ones, teeny-weeny ones—just and otherwise.

PAUL

Tell me some true stories about Dad.

HAROLD

[Unused to the word]

"Dad?"

[Accepting it]

Dad.

[To himself]

The boy wants tales of derring-do. Name a country.

PAUL

England?

HAROLD

[Disgusted]

Oh hell.

PAUL

Dad was never in England?

HAROLD

Behind a desk for a little while.

[Contemptuously]

A desk! They had him planning air raids. A city can't flee like a coward or fight like a man, and the choice between fleeing and fighting was at the core of the life of Harold Ryan. There was only one thing he enjoyed more than watching someone make that choice, and that was making the choice himself. Ask about Spain, where he was the youngest soldier in the Abraham Lincoln Brigade. He was a famous sniper. They called him "La Picadura"—"the sting."

PAUL

[Echoing wonderingly]

"The sting."

HAROLD

As in "Death, where is thy sting?" He killed at least fifty men, wounded hundreds more.

PAUL

[Slightly dismayed at such murderousness]

"The sting."

HAROLD

Ask about the time he and I were parachuted into Yugoslavia to join a guerrilla band—in the war against the Nazis.

PAUL

Tell me that.

HAROLD

I saw your father fight Major Siegfried von Konigswald, the Beast of Yugoslavia, hand to hand.

PAUL

[His excitement rising]

Tell me that! Tell me that!

HAROLD

Hid by day—fought by night. At sunset one day, your father and I, peering through field glasses, saw a black Mercedes draw up to a village inn. It was escorted by two motorcyclists and an armored car. Out of the Mercedes stepped one of the most hateful men in all of history—the Beast of Yugoslavia.

PAUL

Wow.

HAROLD

We blacked our hands and faces. At midnight we crept out of the forest and into the village. The name of the village was Mhravitch. Remember that name!

PAUL

Mhravitch.

HAROLD

We came up behind a sentry, and your father slit his throat before he could utter a sound.

PAUL

[Involuntarily]

Uck.

HAROLD

Don't care for cold steel? A knife is worse than a bullet?

PAUL

I don't know.

HAROLD

The story gets hairier. Should I stop?

PAUL

Go on.

HAROLD

We caught another Kraut alone in a back lane. Your father choked him to death with a length of piano wire. Your father was quite a virtuoso with piano wire. That's nicer than a knife, isn't it—as long as you don't look at the face afterwards. The face turns a curious shade of avocado. I must ask the doctor why that is. At any rate, we stole into the back of the inn, and, with the permission of the management, we poisoned the wine of six Krauts who were carousing there.

PAUL

Where did you get the poison?

HAROLD

We carried cyanide capsules. We were supposed to swallow them in case we were captured. It was your father's opinion that the Krauts needed them more than we did at the time.

PAUL

And one of them was the Beast of Yugoslavia?

HAROLD

The Beast was upstairs, and he came running downstairs, for his men were making loud farewells and last wills and testaments—editorializing about the hospitality they had received. And your father said to him in perfect German, which he had learned in the Spanish Civil War, "Major, something tragic seems to have happened to your body-guard. I am Harold Ryan, of the United States of America. You, I believe, are the Beast of Yugoslavia."

[Blackout]

SCENE SEVEN

SILENCE. Pitch blackness. The sounds of a Nazi rally come up slowly: "Sieg Heil! Sieg Heil! Sieg Heil!" Spotlight comes up on MAJOR SIEGFRIED VON KONIGSWALD, an officer in the dreaded SS. He is in full ceremonial uniform. The sounds fade.

VON KONIGSWALD

[Sadly, resignedly, remembering]

Ja ja. Ja ja.

[Pause]

I am Major Siegfried von Konigswald. They used to call me "The Beast of Yugoslavia," on account of all the people I had tortured and shot—and hanged. We'd bop 'em on the head. We'd hook 'em up to the electricity. We'd stick 'em with hypodermic syringes full of all kinds of stuff. One time we killed a guy with orange juice. There was a train wreck, and two of the freight cars were loaded with oranges, so we had oceans of orange juice. It was a joke—how much orange juice we had. And we were interrogating a guy one day, and he wouldn't talk, and the next thing

I know—somebody's filling up this big syringe with orange juice.

[Pause]

There was a guerrilla war going on. You couldn't tell who was a guerrilla and who wasn't. Even if you got one, it was still a civilian you got. Telling Americans what a guerrilla war is like—that's coals to Newcastle. How do you like that for idiomatic English? "Coals to Newcastle."

[He laughs]

That Harold Ryan—he says he spoke to me in perfect German? He talks German like my ass chews gum. I'm glad to hear the wonderful thing he said before he killed me. I sure didn't understand it the first time around. I figured he was a Lithuanian or something, which will give you an idea of how wrong you can be. All I knew was he was very proud about something, and he had a machine pistol, and it was aimed at me. The woods were full of all kinds of nuts who were proud of some damn thing or other, and they all had guns. They were always looking for revenge. You find a way to bottle revenge—that's the end of Schnapps *und* Coca-Cola.

[Pause]

Harold Ryan said he killed maybe two hundred guys. I killed a hundred times that many, I bet. That's still peanuts, of course, compared to what that crazy Looseleaf did. Harold and me—we was doing it the hard way. I hope the record books will show that. There should be a little star or something by the names of the guys who did it the hard way.

[Pause]

I'm up in Heaven now, like that little Wanda June kid. I wasn't hit by no ice-cream truck. Harold Ryan killed me with his bare hands. He was good. My eyes popped out. My tongue stuck out like a red banana. I shit in my pants. It was a mess.

[Pause]

When I got up on the day I died, I said, "What a beautiful day this is. What a beautiful part of the world." The whole planet was beautiful. Up here I meet guys from other planets.

[He laughs]

We got some really crazy-looking guys up here. Their planets weren't anywhere near as nice as Earth. They had clouds all the time. They never saw a clear blue sky. They never saw snow. They never saw an ocean. They had some little lakes, but you couldn't go swimming in them. The lakes was acid. You go swimming, you dissolve. We got some guys up here who got shoved in them lakes. They dissolved.

[Pause]

Harold Ryan stopped talking German to me there in Yugoslavia. He switched to English, so I finally got some kind of idea what he was so burned up about. He wanted revenge for the guy we killed with orange juice. I don't know how he ever found out about it. There was just three of us there when we did it—me and two regular military doctors. Somebody who cleaned up afterwards must have squealed. If I'd lived through the war, and they tried me for war crimes and all that, I'd have to tell the court, I guess, "I was only following orders, as a good soldier should. Hitler *told* me to kill this guy with orange juice."

[Blackout]

SCENE EIGHT

DARKNESS. Lights come up on living room. HAROLD *has just finished telling his true war story to* PAUL.

HAROLD

Mhravitch. Remember that name.

PAUL

Mhravitch.

HAROLD

The name will live forever. It was there that Harold Ryan slew the Beast of Yugoslavia. Mhravitch.

PAUL

When I grow up, I'm going to go to Mhravitch.

HAROLD

It's rather a disappointment these days. It isn't there any more.

PAUL

Sir?

HAROLD

The Germans shot everybody who lived there, then
leveled it, plowed it, planted turnips and cabbages in the
fertile ground. They wished revenge for the slaying of the
Beast of Yugoslavia. To their twisted way of thinking, your
father had butchered an Eagle Scout.

[Abruptly]

Play lots of contact sports?

PAUL

I wanted to go out for football, but Mom was afraid I'd get
hurt.

HAROLD

You're *supposed* to get hurt!

PAUL

Dr. Woodly says he's seen hundreds of children perma-
nently injured by football. He says that when there's a war,
everybody goes but football players.

HAROLD

Does it bother you to have your mother engaged to a man
like that?

PAUL

They're not engaged.

HAROLD

He seems to think they are. He *told* me they were.

PAUL

Oh no, no, no, no, no. It can't be. How embarrassing.

HAROLD

[Unexpectedly moved]

You're a very good boy to respond that way.

PAUL

No, no, no, no, no.

HAROLD

I'd like to use the sanitary facilities, if I may.

PAUL

Go ahead.

[As HAROLD exits]

No, no, no, no.

[PENELOPE and SHUTTLE enter through the front door. They are tremendously relieved to see PAUL]

PENELOPE

Thank God!

SHUTTLE

What a relief!

PENELOPE

[Going to PAUL]

My baby's safe!

[PAUL *angrily avoids her touch*]

What's the matter now?

SHUTTLE

We got a birthday cake, kid. Did you see the cake?

PAUL

Are you and Dr. Woodly engaged?

PENELOPE

[Stunned]

Who have you been talking to?

PAUL

What difference does that make? Is Dr. Woodly going to be my father now?

[Pause]

PENELOPE

Yes, he is.

PAUL

[A stifled, gargling cry]

Aaaaaaaaaaaaaaaaaah!

SHUTTLE

[Sick]

That goes double for *me*.

PAUL

I don't want to live any more.

SHUTTLE

I feel like I want to yell my head off—just yell anything.

[Yelling]

Bullllllllllllllllllllll-dickey!

PAUL

I'll kill myself.

SHUTTLE

The wife of Harold Ryan is going to marry a pansy next? This is the end of Western Civilization as far as I'm concerned. You must be crazy as a fruitcake.

PENELOPE

Possibly.

SHUTTLE

How long has this been going on?

PENELOPE

A week. We were waiting for the right time to—

SHUTTLE

I feel as though I had been made a perfect chump of.

PENELOPE

I'm sorry.

SHUTTLE

Marry me instead.

PENELOPE

Thank you, Herb. You're a wonderful man. You really are. Everybody respects you for what you've done for scouting and the Little League.

SHUTTLE

You're saying no.

PENELOPE

I'm saying no—and thank you.

SHUTTLE

I didn't make my move fast enough. That's it, isn't it? I was too respectful.

PENELOPE

You were wonderful.

SHUTTLE

What's so wonderful if I lost the sale?

[Turning to PAUL]

You poor kid.

PAUL

Don't touch me.

SHUTTLE

Wouldn't you rather have your mother marry me than him?

PAUL

No.

SHUTTLE

[Moving dazedly toward the front door]

All my dreams have suddenly collapsed.

[Pause]

We did have a lot of laughs together, Penelope.

PENELOPE

It's true.

SHUTTLE

Well—it was nice while it lasted. Thanks for the memories.

[He exits,

Silence. A toilet flushes loudly and complicatedly]

PENELOPE

Is Norbert still here?

PAUL

No.

PENELOPE

Then who flushed the toilet?

PAUL

Father's friend.

PENELOPE

What's his name?

PAUL

Don't know.

PENELOPE

For Heaven sakes!

[HAROLD enters, still adjusting his trousers]

How do you do?

HAROLD

How do *you* do, Mrs. Ryan? I'd heard you were beautiful, and so you are. Am I intruding here?

PENELOPE

Not at all.

HAROLD

I couldn't help overhearing that you were about to get married again.

[PENELOPE has now recognized him, but attempts to protect herself from shock by pretending that she has not]

PENELOPE

Our family physician has asked me to marry him. Paul needs the guidance and companionship that only a man can give. He isn't at all like Harold. But then again, I'm not the woman I was eight years ago.

[She slumps into a chair, buries her face in her hands]

PAUL

Mom?

PENELOPE

[Pointing weakly]

That man is your father.

PAUL

What?

PENELOPE

There stand the loins from which you've sprung.

PAUL

I don't get it.

PENELOPE

It *is* you, isn't it, Harold?

HAROLD

[Enjoying the drama hugely]

Yes, wife, it is.

[To PAUL]

Come here, boy. Your father is home.

PAUL

Sir?

PENELOPE

Go to him.

[PAUL goes to HAROLD dazedly. They embrace clumsily]

HAROLD	PAUL
Son, son, son. . . .	Father, father, father. . . .

[They part, unsatisfied and confused. HAROLD goes to PENELOPE, his arms outstretched]

HAROLD

Wife, wife, wife. . . .

[PENELOPE struggles to her feet, her face blank. HAROLD embraces her, finds himself wrestling with a rigid, unresponsive object]

Wife, wife, wife. . . .

[HAROLD lets go, backs away from her]

What's the matter?

PENELOPE

[Tearful]

Give us time.

HAROLD

Like hugging a lamp post.

PENELOPE

Give us time, Harold—to adjust to your being alive.

HAROLD

You were well adjusted to my being dead?

PENELOPE

We adjust to what there is to adjust to. Perhaps Paul, being young, can adjust to joy or grief immediately. I

hope he can. I will take a little longer. I'll be as quick as
I can.

HAROLD

What sort of time period do you have in mind? Half an
hour? An hour?

PENELOPE

I don't know. This is a new disease to me.

HAROLD

Disease?

PENELOPE

Situation.

HAROLD

This reunion isn't what I imagined it would be.

PENELOPE

A telegram—a phone call might have helped.

HAROLD

Seemed the most honest way to begin life together again—
natural, unrehearsed.

PENELOPE

Well—enjoy the natural, honest, unrehearsed result—
surgical shock.

HAROLD

You feel that you're behaving as a woman should?

PENELOPE

Every fuse in my nervous system has been blown.

[*Lion doorbell roars*]

Who's that? Teddy Roosevelt?

[PAUL *answers the door, admits* WOODLY]

WOODLY

[*To* PAUL]

Safe and sound, I see.

[*To* HAROLD]

Oh—you came back.

HAROLD

I came back.

PENELOPE

You *know* each other?

WOODLY

We met here earlier this evening.

PENELOPE

How neat. How keen.

HAROLD

How was the emergency, Doctor? Profitable, I hope.

WOODLY

A policeman delivered the baby in a taxicab.

HAROLD

Tough luck. You'll have to split the fee.

WOODLY

[*Puzzled by* PENELOPE's *mood*]

Are—are you *crying*, Penelope?

HAROLD

She's crying because she's so happy.

PENELOPE

That's why I'm crying.

PAUL

Dr. Woodly?

[*Indicating* HAROLD]

You know who this is?

WOODLY

I didn't get his name. A friend of your father?

PAUL

He isn't any friend of Father.

WOODLY

He isn't?

PAUL

He *is* my father.

WOODLY

No!

PENELOPE

Eeeeeeeeeeee-*yup*. Dr. Woodly—I would like you to meet Harold, my husband. Harold, this is Dr. Woodly, my fiancé.

[She crosses to the door of the master bedroom, kissing each male lightly as she passes]

Good night, dear. Good night, dear.

[She stands in the doorway]

Stay or go, talk or sulk, laugh or cry—as you wish. Do whatever seems called for. My mind is gone. Good night.

[She exits into bedroom, closes the door firmly, locks it audibly]

WOODLY

[Dazedly]

I feel the same way. What next?

HAROLD

What next? You leave promptly, of course. There is no question as to whose home this is—

WOODLY

None.

HAROLD

Whose son this is, whose wife that is. A fiancé is the most ridiculous appurtenance this household could have at this time. Good night.

WOODLY

[Crushed, without any possible comeback]

Good night.

[He exits through the front door. HAROLD *goes at once to* PENELOPE'S *door, tries it, finds it locked]*

HAROLD

Penelope! God damn it! Penelope!

[He considers kicking down the door, thinks better of this, turns away]

Wants to fix up her makeup, no doubt.

PAUL

Is Looseleaf Harper alive?

HAROLD

Alive and hale. He's throwing a little surprise party for his own family. Is your mother often this unstable?

[Not waiting for an answer, calling again]

Penelope!

PAUL

She's a real heavy sleeper sometimes.

HAROLD

Why don't you go to bed—son.

PAUL

I can't take my eyes off you.

HAROLD

Tomorrow's another day.

PAUL

You know what my English literature teacher said about you?

HAROLD

Can't it keep till morning?

PAUL

She said you were *legendary.* I wrote a theme about you, and she said, "Your father is a legendary hero out of the Golden Age of Heroes."

HAROLD

That's nice. You thank her for me. Go to bed and get lots of sleep, and then you thank her in the morning.

PAUL

Tomorrow's Saturday. Anyway, she's dead.

HAROLD

Penelope!

PAUL

She was killed in the park two months ago—in the day-time.

HAROLD

Penelope!

PAUL

She was on her way home from a meeting of the African Violet Society, and they got her.

HAROLD

[Sharply]

Will you go to bed?

PAUL

[Stung]

Yes sir. If you can't wake Mom up, I've got double-decker bunks.

HAROLD

[Stamping his foot]

Scat!

[PAUL exits hastily down the corridor to his room. HAROLD goes to PENELOPE's door, attempts to woo her through it]

Penelope—darling—can you hear me? Wife—you know what kept me alive all these fevered, swampy, nightmare years? Your heavenly face, Penelope, my wife—shimmering before me, coaxing me up from my knees, begging me to stagger one step closer to home. Has love ever reached so far? Has love ever overcome more hardships than mine?

[Silence]

Has love ever asked more manliness of a man, more womanliness of a woman? Has ever a man done more for a woman's reward?

[The bedroom door opens, revealing PENELOPE]

PENELOPE

[Hollowly, to the world at large]

There is no one in here of any earthly use to anyone tonight. Tomorrow is another day.
[She closes the door and locks it]

HAROLD

[To audience]

End of Act One.

[Blackout]

ACT TWO

SCENE ONE

DARKNESS. PAUL, *alone in the living room, hammers on his mother's door. He wears pajamas.*

PAUL

Mom! Mother! Mom!

[Toilet flushes. Lights come up on the living room. It is morning]

Dad's got jungle fever, Mom. What'll I do? Mom!

HAROLD

[A moment of exhaustion]

Damn.

PAUL

Mom?

[Door to the master bedroom opens. PENELOPE *appears in the doorway. She has decided during an almost sleepless night that she*

owes it to PAUL *and to her own self-respect to explore the possibility of beginning her life with* HAROLD *anew. She is terrified of him. She hopes that if she can keep calm and open her fears will diminish. Perhaps she can love him again]*

PENELOPE

[Attempting to behave mechanically as a good wife should]

What are his symptoms?

PAUL

Shivers and sweats and groans. His teeth chatter. What'll we do?

PENELOPE

What does *he* say to do?

PAUL

He can hardly talk.

HAROLD

[Responding to a last twinge of nausea]

Bluh.

PENELOPE

You'd better get Dr. Woodly.

PAUL

Really?

PENELOPE

It *is* an emergency, isn't it?

PAUL

[Uncertainly]

Yeah.

PENELOPE

Then get him.

PAUL

[Thinking she has made a mistake]

Okay.

[He exits through front door, leaves door open. We hear him knocking on a door in the hallway]

Dr. Woodly?

[HAROLD enters, drained but recovering. He chews on a root. He has slept in the shirt and trousers he wore the night before. He is barefoot. PAUL knocks again]

Dr. Woodly?

[There is the sound of WOODLY's door opening. WOODLY and PAUL speak unintelligibly, WOODLY evidently inviting PAUL in for a moment. WOODLY's door closes]

HAROLD

What's that all about?

PENELOPE

We thought a doctor might help.

HAROLD

Your old beau?

PENELOPE

We thought it was an emergency.

HAROLD

I don't want that chancre mechanic in here.

PENELOPE

He's a very decent man, Harold.

HAROLD

We all are.

PENELOPE

Shouldn't you lie down?

HAROLD

When I'm dead—

[Throwing it away]

or fucking.

PENELOPE

Paul said you were awfully sick.

HAROLD

I was, I was. It never lasts long.

[He hears WOODLY's door open, is alert to WOODLY's approach, continues to speak to PENELOPE absently]

The Indians call it "Zamba-keetya"—the little cloudburst.

[WOODLY and PAUL enter. WOODLY is correctly professional and carries a little black bag]

WOODLY

Ah! You're ambulatory!

HAROLD

What a brilliant diagnosis!

PENELOPE

You know what I want?

[All look at her]

I want you both to be friends. I know you both, respect you both. You *should* be friends.

HAROLD

Nothing would please me more.

PENELOPE

[Believing him]

Thank God!

WOODLY

[Pleased but careful]

Well now—what seems to be the trouble with the patient today? A touch of malaria, perhaps?

HAROLD

I know malaria. Malaria isn't caused by the bites of bats.

WOODLY

You've been bitten by bats?

HAROLD

Colonel Harper and I once shared a treetop with a family of bats. There was a flash flood. There were piranha fish in the water. That's how Colonel Harper lost his little toe.

WOODLY

You have chills?

HAROLD

Chills, fevers, sweats. You can describe it and name it after yourself: "the Woodly galloping crud."

[WOODLY enjoys the joke and the blooming friendship]

You can also describe its cure. I'm eating its cure.

WOODLY

I was going to ask.

HAROLD

Pacqualinincheewa root.

WOODLY

Would you say that again?

HAROLD

Pacqualinincheewa root. Means "cougar fang." Cures anything but a yellow streak down the back.

WOODLY

I've never heard of it.

HAROLD

Congratulations. By crossing twenty-eight feet of cockroach-infested carpet, you've become the third white man ever to hear of it.

WOODLY

[Fascinated]

And you've seen it work cures?

HAROLD

Hundreds.

PENELOPE

I'm so glad you like each other. I was so scared, so scared.

HAROLD

[Breaking off a piece, offering it]

Have some.

WOODLY

Thank you. Thank you very much.

PENELOPE

I believe in miracles now.

HAROLD

Wasn't that sweet of me?

WOODLY

More and more we find ourselves laying aside false pride and looking into the pharmacopoeias of primitive people. Curare, ephedrine—we've found some amazing things.

HAROLD

We have, have we?

WOODLY

That's an editorial *we,* of course. I haven't turned up anything personally.

HAROLD

Everything about you is the editorial *we.* Take that away from you, and you'd disappear.

PENELOPE

Harold!

HAROLD

I could carve a better man out of a banana!

PENELOPE

Please—

HAROLD

You and your damned bedside manner and your damned little black bag full of miracles. You know who filled that bag for you? Not Alice-sit-by-the-fires like yourself. Men with guts filled it, by God—men with guts enough to pay the price for miracles—suffering, ingratitude, loneliness, death—

WOODLY

[Off balance]

Good Lord.

HAROLD

I can just hear the editorial wee-wee-weeing when Looseleaf and I start flying in pacqualinincheewa root. I can hear
the Alice-sit-by-the-fires now: "We discovered it in the
Amazon Rain Forest. Now we cure you with it. Now we
lower our eyes with becoming modesty as we receive
heartfelt thanks."

[HAROLD *suddenly goes to* WOODLY, *takes his hand and pretends
abject gratitude*]

Oh, bless you, Doctor, bless you—oh healer, oh protector,
oh giver of life.

[WOODLY *withdraws his hand, examines it as though it were
diseased*]

PENELOPE

He doesn't *deserve* this! You don't know him. It isn't fair!

HAROLD

He thought he could take my place. It is now my privilege
to give an unambiguous account of why I don't think he's
man enough to do that.

WOODLY

I thought she was a widow.

HAROLD

You were wrong, you quack!

PENELOPE

Awful.

[Approaching WOODLY, but not getting too close]

I can't tell you how sorry I am.

HAROLD

Say hello to your mother.

PENELOPE

[Fervently]

Do say hello to your mother.

WOODLY

I'm taking her to the airport a few minutes from now. She's going to East St. Louis—to visit an aunt.

PENELOPE

Tell her to have a nice trip.

WOODLY

[Moving toward the front door]

Thanks.

[HAROLD laughs. This stings WOODLY to a cold, peace-loving anger]

I'm going to have to report you to the Department of Health.

HAROLD

What for?

WOODLY

Quarantine, possibly. You may be suffering from a loathsome disease which the American people could do without. Goodbye.

[He exits instantly]

HAROLD

Now that's what I call fun.

PENELOPE

Ghastly, cruel, unnecessary.

HAROLD

You'll get so you enjoy twitting weaklings again. You used to eat it up.

PENELOPE

I did?

HAROLD

We were one hell of a pair—and we'll be one again. What we need is a honeymoon. Let's start right now.

PENELOPE

A trip, you mean?

HAROLD

I *had* a trip. We'll honeymoon here.

[To PAUL]

Go out and play.

PAUL

Play?

HAROLD

Your mother and I do not wish to be disturbed for three full hours.

PENELOPE

He hasn't had breakfast yet.

HAROLD

Buy yourself breakfast.

[He takes his billfold from his hip pocket, hands PAUL *a $100 bill]*

There we go.

PAUL

A hundred dollars!

HAROLD

The smallest thing I've got.

PAUL

Can I get dressed first?

HAROLD

Make it fast.

*[*PAUL *exits to his bedroom.* HAROLD *turns to* PENELOPE*]*

Honeymoon! Honeymoon! Say it: *Honeymoon!*

PENELOPE

It's so—so *stark.*

HAROLD

You used to like it stark!

PENELOPE

Just—*bang*—we have a honeymoon.

HAROLD

[Beginning to stalk her cunningly]

I'm not going to strike you. I am going to be as gentle as pie—as lemon meringue pie. You mustn't run away now. This is your loving husband approaching. I'm your husband. Society approves!

[PENELOPE wants to run, but doesn't]

Good! You held your ground.

[HAROLD is very close now, but not touching her]

Now—turn around, if you would.

PENELOPE

Turn *around*?

HAROLD

[Laughing]

I'm not about to introduce to you a jungle novelty. What I have in mind is massage—a perfectly decent massage. Turn around, turn around.

[PENELOPE obeys]

I'm going to touch your shoulders very gently now. You mustn't scream.

[He touches her shoulders gently, expertly]

So tense, so tense.

PENELOPE

You shouldn't have talked to Norbert that way.

HAROLD

You're thinking with your brain instead of your body. That's why you're so tense! Forget Norbert. Relax. It's body time.

PENELOPE

I have a brain.

HAROLD

We all do. But now it's body time. Relax. Ideally, the body of a woman should feel like a hot water bottle filled with Devonshire cream. You feel like a paper bag crammed with curtain rods. Think of your muscles one by one. Let them go slack. Relax. Let the brain go blank. Relax. That's the idea—that's my girl. Now the small of the back. Let those knots over those kidneys unsnarl.

PAUL

[Entering, dressed to go out and play]

Dad—

HAROLD

[Hanging on to PENELOPE, *but knowing the mood has been broken]*

Couldn't you have vanished quietly out the back door?

PAUL

A hundred dollars for breakfast?

HAROLD

Leave a tip.

PENELOPE

[Suddenly twisting away, having been nearly hypnotized]

I have some change.

HAROLD

Ram it up your ass!

[He realizes at once that his violent side has severely damaged the side of him which is the great seducer. PENELOPE and PAUL are straight as ramrods]

I *do* beg your pardon.

[Sincerely]

Those words were illy chosen. There is tension in *all* of us here. Something you must both understand, however, is that the head of this household is home, and he is Harold Ryan, and people do what he says when he says it. That's the way this particular clock is constructed.

[Lion doorbell roars]

Sometimes even I hate that thing.

[PAUL goes reeling to the door in terror, admits LOOSELEAF, who has also been sleeping in his clothes]

LOOSELEAF

[Walking right in]

I've been looking at motorcycles.

HAROLD

Go home!

LOOSELEAF

You ever own a motorcycle?

HAROLD

[To PENELOPE]

You're right! We'll take a trip. A trip is what we'll take.

[To LOOSELEAF]

I don't want to talk about motorcycles. I don't want to talk about tits. Go home!

LOOSELEAF

Haven't got one.

PENELOPE

[To LOOSELEAF]

And you went home unannounced, too?

LOOSELEAF

I dunno. Yeah! Yeah! Yeah! I did.

HAROLD

And how were things?

LOOSELEAF

Let's talk about something else.

PENELOPE

[To HAROLD]

Alice got married again.

LOOSELEAF

She *did*?

PENELOPE

You didn't even find *that* out?

LOOSELEAF

There was so much going on.

PENELOPE

She married an accountant named Stanley Kestenbaum.

LOOSELEAF

So that's it! "Kestenbaum, Kestenbaum." Everybody was yelling "Kestenbaum, Kestenbaum." I thought it was some foreign language.

HAROLD

Otherwise, how are things?

LOOSELEAF

I sure didn't expect her to drop dead.

PENELOPE

Dead!

LOOSELEAF

Jesus.

PENELOPE

[Sick]

Alice is dead?

LOOSELEAF

No, no—shit no.

[He stops short]

Excuse me, Penelope.

PENELOPE

For what?

LOOSELEAF

For saying "shit." Or is that okay now?

PENELOPE

[Shrilly]

Who's dead?

LOOSELEAF

My mother-in-law. Fire engines, pulmotors, doctors, cops, coroners—

PENELOPE

What happened?

LOOSELEAF

Well—I walked up to the front door. I was still alive. Big surprise. I rang the doorbell, and old Mrs. Wheeler answered. She had her Goddamn knitting. I said, "Guess who?" She conked right out.

PENELOPE

How horrible.

LOOSELEAF

Yeah—cripes. I never did get any sense out of Alice. She found me holding up the old lady, dead as a mackerel. It was a bitch. You know—maybe Mrs. Wheeler was going to die then and there anyway, even if I'd been the paper boy. Maybe not. I dunno, boy. That's civilian life for you. Who knows what kills anybody?

HAROLD

Could have happened to anybody.

LOOSELEAF

First Nagasaki—now this.

HAROLD

How about breakfast, wife?

PENELOPE

Breakfast?

HAROLD

[As though to a waitress]

Scrambled eggs, kippered herring, fried potatoes—and a whole onion. I want to eat the onion like an apple. Do you understand?

[PENELOPE turns away]

And lots of orange juice—oceans of orange juice.

PENELOPE

Mrs. Wheeler is dead.

HAROLD

All right—bring me a side order of Mrs. Wheeler.

[Regarding LOOSELEAF, resigning himself to being stuck with his company for a little while longer]

Oh hell—sit down, Colonel. Penelope will bring you some chow.

PENELOPE

That is the most heartless statement I ever heard pass between human lips.

HAROLD

[Honestly mystified]

Which one?

PENELOPE

[Chokingly]

"Bring me a side order of Mrs. Wheeler."

HAROLD

She's up in Heaven now. She didn't hear. She is experiencing nothing but pure happiness. There's nothing nicer than that.

[Suddenly, angrily, slamming a table with his fist]

Chow! Harold Ryan wants chow!

PENELOPE

What a honeymoon.

HAROLD

Honeymoon temporarily canceled.

[Catching sight of PAUL, whose physical appearance really offends him]

The boy should still go out and exercise. I have the impression he never gets any exercise. He simply bloats himself with Fig Newtons and bakes his brains over steam radiators.

PENELOPE

You're wrong.

HAROLD

Then let me see him go out and get some exercise.

[Explosively]

Right now!

[PAUL goes reeling in terror to the front door, opens it]

PAUL

[To HAROLD, abjectly]

What *kind* of exercise?

HAROLD

Beat the shit out of someone who hates you.

[PAUL exits. HAROLD pounds on a table]

Chow, chow, chow! God damn it—nutriment!

PENELOPE

We're all going to have to go out for breakfast. The cook quit yesterday.

HAROLD

You're a woman, aren't you?

[PENELOPE *nods*]

Then we *have* a cook.

[PENELOPE *hesitates*]

Cook, by God! Cook! You're the nigger now.

PENELOPE

People don't use that word any more.

HAROLD

Don't lecture me on race relations. I don't have a molecule of prejudice. I've been in battle with every kind of man there is. I've been in bed with every kind of woman there is—from a Laplander to a Tierra del Fuegian. If I'd ever been to the South Pole, there'd be a hell of a lot of penguins who looked like me. Cook!

PENELOPE

You leave me so—so without—without *dignity*.

HAROLD

People now have dignity when frying eggs?

PENELOPE

They don't have to feel like slaves.

HAROLD

[Grandly]

Then go now—and fry with dignity—sunnyside up.

[PENELOPE attempts to respond to this, but is too enraged. She exits, making a tiny mosquito-like hum]

LOOSELEAF

I dunno, boy.

HAROLD

The educational process.

LOOSELEAF

I guess. You're lucky you don't have any old people around here.

HAROLD

She was about to get married again. She locked me out of the bedroom last night.

[LOOSELEAF starts to laugh. HAROLD shuts him up]

What's funny about that?

LOOSELEAF

[Apologetically]

You know me, boy.

[PENELOPE enters from the kitchen with a question on her lips]

HAROLD

I should have torn that door off its hinges. Should have scrogged her ears off. Should have broken the bed.

[Seeing PENELOPE*]*

What do *you* want?

[Words fail her]

Well?

PENELOPE

I—I was wondering—is there anything you shouldn't eat—because of jungle fever?

HAROLD

I could eat a raw baby crocodile.

[Turning to LOOSELEAF *crassly]*

The way to get your wife back is in bed. Do such a job on her that she'll be lucky if she can crawl around on all fours.

[To PENELOPE*]*

We're starving. Do you mind?

*[*PENELOPE *exits dumbly, detesting the word "scrog," which she has never heard before]*

She had two lovers, by the way.

*[*LOOSELEAF *starts to laugh again, stops the laugh as* HAROLD *glowers]*

LOOSELEAF

Excuse me.

HAROLD

One of them is the doctor, whose weapons are compassion, unselfishness, peacefulness—maudlin concern.

LOOSELEAF

Huh.

HAROLD

He and his love are like a retiarius. Do you know what a retiarius is?

LOOSELEAF

He's a kind of gladiator who fights with a knife and a net and doesn't wear anything but a jockstrap.

HAROLD

[Amazed]

How do you know that?

LOOSELEAF

You told me.

HAROLD

When?

LOOSELEAF

When we were up in the tree so long—with the bats.

HAROLD

Oh. I'd forgotten.

LOOSELEAF

Fourteen times you told me. I counted.

HAROLD

Really?

LOOSELEAF

You'd get this funny look in your eyes, and I'd say to myself, "Oh, Jesus—he's going to tell me what a retiarius is again."

HAROLD

[Acknowledging a flaw in a manly way]

Sorry.

[PENELOPE enters, is about to speak. HAROLD stops her with a raised finger]

Let me guess—breakfast is served?

PENELOPE

No.

HAROLD

What then?

PENELOPE

I do not wish to be *scrogged*—ever. I never heard that word, but when I heard it, I knew it was one thing I never wanted to have happen to me.

HAROLD

That's what you're *supposed* to say.

PENELOPE

This is not a coy deception. I do not want to be scrogged.
I want love. I want tenderness.

HAROLD

You don't *know* what you want. That's the way God *built*
you!

PENELOPE

I will not be scrogged. I remember one time I saw you
wrench a hook from the throat of a fish with a pair of
pliers, and you promised me that the fish couldn't feel.

HAROLD

It couldn't!

PENELOPE

I'd like to have the expert opinion of the fish—along with
yours.

HAROLD

[Shaking his head]

Fish can't feel.

PENELOPE

Well, *I* can. Some injuries, spiritual or physical, can be
excruciating to me. I'm not a silly carhop any more.

[An unexpected, minor insight]

Maybe you're right about fish. When I was a carhop,
I didn't feel much more than a fish would. But I've been
sensitized. I have ideas now—and solid information.

I know a lot more now—and a lot of it has to do with *you*.

HAROLD

[*Sensing danger*]

Such as? . . .

PENELOPE

The whole concept of heroism—and its sexual roots.

HAROLD

Tell me about its sexual roots.

PENELOPE

It's complicated and I don't want to go into it now, because it's bound to sound insulting—even though nobody means for anybody to be insulted. It's just the truth.

HAROLD

I like the truth. I wouldn't be alive today if I weren't one of the biggest fans truth ever had.

PENELOPE

Well—part of it is that heroes basically hate home and never stay there very long, and make awful messes while they're there.

HAROLD

Go on.

PENELOPE

[*Blurting*]

And they have very mixed feelings about women. They hate them in a way. One reason they like war so much is that they can capture enemy women and not have to make love to them slowly and gently. They can *scrog* them, as you say—

[Pause]

for revenge.

HAROLD

You learned this in some college course?

PENELOPE

I learned a lot of things in college. Actually—it was Norbert who told me that.

HAROLD

[Darkly]

The doctor.

PENELOPE

Yes.

HAROLD

And what is his most cherished possession?

PENELOPE

[Not sensing the drift of the conversation]

His most cherished possession? His violin, I guess.

HAROLD

And he keeps it in his apartment?

PENELOPE

[Still at sea]

Yes.

HAROLD

And no one's there now?

PENELOPE

I don't think so.

HAROLD

That's too bad. I would rather have him at home—to *see* what I'm going to do.

PENELOPE

[Suddenly catching on, sick with fear]

What are you going to do?

HAROLD

He did his best to destroy my most precious possession, which is the high opinion women have of me. I'm now going to even that score. I'm going to break in his door and I'm going to smash his violin.

PENELOPE

No you're not!

HAROLD

Why not?

PENELOPE

Because if you do—I'll *leave* you.

HAROLD

[Promptly and emotionlessly]

Goodbye.

[Blackout]

SCENE TWO

Spotlight comes up on VON KONIGSWALD *and* WANDA JUNE, *dressed as before. They have become close friends.*

WANDA JUNE

We have this new club up here in Heaven.

VON KONIGSWALD

Yes, we do.

WANDA JUNE

We only have two members so far, but it's growing all the time.

VON KONIGSWALD

We have enough for a shuffleboard team. In Heaven, shuffleboard is everything. Hitler plays shuffleboard.

WANDA JUNE

Albert Einstein plays shuffleboard.

VON KONIGSWALD

Mozart plays shuffleboard.

WANDA JUNE

Lewis Carroll, who wrote *Alice in Wonderland,* plays shuffleboard.

VON KONIGSWALD

Jack the Ripper plays shuffleboard.

WANDA JUNE

Walt Disney, who gave us *Snow White and the Seven Dwarfs,* plays shuffleboard. Jesus Christ plays shuffleboard.

VON KONIGSWALD

It was almost worth the trip—to find out that Jesus Christ in Heaven was just another guy, playing shuffleboard. I like his sense of humor, though—you know? He's got a blue-and-gold warm-up jacket he wears. You know what it says on the back? "Pontius Pilate Athletic Club." Most people don't get it. Most people think there really is a Pontius Pilate Athletic Club.

WANDA JUNE

We're going to have jackets, aren't we?

VON KONIGSWALD

You bet! "The Harold Ryan Fan Club." Pink, eh? With a yellow streak up the back.

[BOTH *laugh*]

We got very good tailor shops up here. They'll make you any kind of uniform, any kind of sweatsuit you want. Judas Iscariot—he's got this black jacket with a skull and cross-bones over the heart. He walks around all hunched over, and he never looks anybody in the eye, and written on the back of his jacket are the words, "Go take a flying—

[WANDA JUNE *punches him in the ribs*]

leap at the moon."

[MILDRED, HAROLD's *third wife, enters. She is voluptuous, blowzy, tough—about forty-five. She has trouble with alcohol.* VON KONIGSWALD *is expecting her*]

Aha! Hello! You're Mildred, right?

MILDRED

I heard you were looking for me.

VON KONIGSWALD

You were Harold Ryan's third wife. Right?

MILDRED

Yes.

VON KONIGSWALD

You want to join the Harold Ryan Fan Club? Wear a pink jacket with a yellow streak up the back?

MILDRED

Do I have to? Who's the little girl?

WANDA JUNE

Mr. Ryan just borrowed my birthday cake. I don't really know him.

MILDRED

Thought you were another wife, maybe.

WANDA JUNE

I'm only *ten* years old.

MILDRED

That's what he wanted—a ten-year-old wife. He'd come home from a war or a safari, and he'd wind up talking to the little kids.

WANDA JUNE

Won't you *please* join our club? Please?

MILDRED

Honey—Alcoholics Anonymous takes all the time I've got—and Harold Ryan is an individual I would rather forget. He drove me to drink. He drove his first two wives to drink.

VON KONIGSWALD

Because he was cruel?

MILDRED

[Covering WANDA JUNE's *little ears*]

Premature ejaculation.

VON KONIGSWALD

Ach sooooooooooooo.

MILDRED

No grown woman is a fan of premature ejaculation. Harold would come home trumpeting and roaring. He would kick the furniture with his boots, spit into corners and the fireplace. He would make me presents of stuffed fish and helmets with holes in them. He would tell me that he had now earned the reward that only a woman could give him, and he'd tear off my clothes. He would carry me into the bedroom, telling me to scream and kick my feet. That was very important to him. I did it. I tried to be a good wife. He told me to imagine a herd of stampeding water buffalo. I couldn't do that, but I pretended I did. It was all over—ten seconds after he'd said the word "buffalo." Then he'd zip up his pants, and go outside, and tell true war stories to the little kids. Any little kids.

VON KONIGSWALD

That is sad.

MILDRED

[Blankly]

Is it?

[Pause]

I have this theory about why men kill each other and break things.

VON KONIGSWALD

Ja?

MILDRED

Never mind. It's a dumb theory. I was going to say it was all sexual . . . but everything is sexual . . . but alcohol.

[Making peace sign]

Peace.

VON KONIGSWALD & WANDA JUNE

[Making peace signs]

Peace.

[Blackout]

SCENE THREE

Silence. Darkness.

WOODY WOODPECKER VOICE

Ha ha ha *ha* ha!

[Pistol shot]

You got me, pal.

[Silence. A baby cries. Silence. The lights come up]

LOOSELEAF

Go to the *funeral*?

HAROLD

Of course! Not only go to it but go to it in full uniform!
Rent a uniform!

LOOSELEAF

That's against the law, isn't it? I can't wear a uniform
anymore.

HAROLD

Wear your uniform and every decoration, and let them despise you, if they dare.

LOOSELEAF

Alice would be absolutely tear-ass.

HAROLD

When I was a naïve young recruit in Spain, I used to wonder why soldiers bayoneted oil paintings, shot the noses off of statues and defecated into grand pianos. I now understand: It was to teach civilians the deepest sort of respect for men in uniform—uncontrollable fear.

[He raises his glass]

To our women.

LOOSELEAF

I didn't know we had any women left.

HAROLD

The world is teeming with women—ours to enjoy.

LOOSELEAF

Every time I start thinking like that I get the clap.

[Lion doorbell roars]

HAROLD

[Going to the door]

This could be my next wife.

[He admits HERB SHUTTLE, who carries a bouquet of roses]

SHUTTLE

[Puzzled by HAROLD]

Hello.

HAROLD

How are you, honeybunch?

SHUTTLE

Is Penelope in?

HAROLD

The posies are for *her*?

SHUTTLE

I wanted to apologize.

HAROLD

You've come to the right man.

SHUTTLE

I forgot my vacuum cleaner.

HAROLD

I forget mine for years on end.

SHUTTLE

[Suddenly realizing who HAROLD is]

Oh my God—

[Pause. SHUTTLE points]

And *you* are Looseleaf Harper.

LOOSELEAF

Hi.

[SHUTTLE *faints*]

HAROLD

[*Crowing*]

It's what I've dreamed of all my life, Looseleaf! To have a grown man realize who I was—and *faint*!

[*To audience*]

End of Act Two.

[*Blackout*]

ACT THREE

MILDRED enters drunkenly up aisle, sits precariously on apron of stage and speaks to audience.

MILDRED

Two days later. The afternoon of the day of Looseleaf Harper's mother-in-law's funeral. You got it? Two days later.

[Pause]

You know what happened in *Heaven* today? There was a tornado. I'm not kidding you—there was a Goddamn tornado. Tore up fifty-six houses, a dance pavilion and a Ferris wheel. Drove a shuffleboard stick clear through a telephone pole. Nobody got killed. Nobody ever gets killed. They just bounce around a lot. Then they get up—and start playing shuffleboard again.

[Pause]

I never saw a tornado when I was alive, and I grew up in Oklahoma. There's this big, black, funnel-shaped cloud. Sounds like a railroad train without the whistle. I had to

137

come to Heaven to see a thing like that. A lot of people got photographs.

[Pause]

After the tornado was over, a man had some film left and he wanted to take pictures of me—to use up the *roll*. I don't like people who go around taking pictures of everything. Nothing's real to some people unless they've got photographs.

[Pause]

Two days later—right?

[She exits clumsily, the way she came. Silence. Lights come up on the living room, which has become a pigpen. LOOSELEAF, HAROLD, SHUTTLE, and PAUL sit around a dinner of nearly raw beefsteak set on the coffee table. LOOSELEAF wears an ill-fitting uniform, which he has rented]

LOOSELEAF

I told you the uniform wouldn't help.

HAROLD

It helped more than you know. Down deep, people were deeply affected.

LOOSELEAF

You keep on saying "deep" and "deeply." I wish something good would happen on the surface sometime.

SHUTTLE

I can't get over how you guys are my friends. Harold Ryan and Looseleaf Harper are my friends.

HAROLD

Our pleasure.

SHUTTLE

Eight years you guys were together—through thick and thin.

HAROLD

For seven and a half of those years we were heavily drugged—or we would have been home long before now, believe me. We were saved from starvation by the Lupi-Loopo Indians, who fed us a strange blue soup.

SHUTTLE

Blue soup.

HAROLD

It sapped our will—made us peaceful and unenterprising. It was a form of chemical castration. We became two more sleepy Indians.

LOOSELEAF

[To PAUL]

So, kid—how they hanging? Or don't you *say* that to a little kid?

HAROLD

He's a *man*.

[To PAUL]

Tell him you're a *man*.

PAUL

I'm a man.

HAROLD

We've got to do something to make this boy's voice change. I wonder if we couldn't get bull balls somewhere, and fry 'em up.

[To PAUL]

Still miss your mother?

PAUL

[Weakly]

No.

HAROLD

You're free to go to her, if you want. If you'd rather be a woman and run with the women, just say the word.

SHUTTLE

Are we really going to find out where the elephants go to die?

HAROLD

I'd rather go to Viet Nam.

SHUTTLE

Would somebody please pass me the catsup?

HAROLD

What you say is, "Pass the fucking catsup."

SHUTTLE

Pass the fucking catsup.

[LOOSELEAF gives it to him. SHUTTLE dumps catsup on his steak]

I keep thinking about Africa—and the elephants.

LOOSELEAF

I don't think I'll go.

HAROLD

Of course you'll go! You're going to fly the helicopter.

LOOSELEAF

I dunno.

HAROLD

You're so *low*! Look at that beautiful red meat. You haven't touched it.

LOOSELEAF

Sorry. At least you've got a place to come back to. I don't have a place to come *back* to anymore.

HAROLD

All the more reason to go to Africa.

LOOSELEAF

I dunno. You know.

[Pause]

I used to really love that Alice. Do you know that?

HAROLD

You know her for what she is now—garbage.

LOOSELEAF

I dunno.

HAROLD

She was always a rotten wife! She was against everything manly you ever wanted to do.

[To SHUTTLE]

He was the most daring test pilot in the country at one time, and his wife made him quit. She made him become a life insurance salesman instead.

SHUTTLE

I'd think any woman worth her salt would be proud to be married to a test pilot. I know I would.

LOOSELEAF

She *tried* to like it. She was a very nervous woman.

SHUTTLE

I could tell that at the funeral.

[To PAUL]

Would you please pass the fucking catsup again? Was it dangerous testing planes?

LOOSELEAF

I dunno. Who knows? You know—you're up there, and you're in some plane nobody ever flew before. You put her into a dive, and everything starts screaming and shaking, and maybe some pipe breaks and squirts oil or gasoline or hydraulic fluid in your face. You wonder how the hell you ever got in such a mess, and then you pull back on the controls, and you black out for a couple of seconds. When you come to, everything's usually fairly okay—except maybe you threw up all over yourself. It's just another job, but you try and tell Alice that.

HAROLD

Insurance!

SHUTTLE

You actually *sold* insurance?

LOOSELEAF

I tried.

[Indicating HAROLD]

I sold *him* some. That was the only insurance I ever sold.

[Hyena doorbell laughs]

SHUTTLE

What an awful sound!

HAROLD

Get used to it.

[To PAUL]

Back door, Paul.

[PAUL exits to the kitchen. To SHUTTLE]

It's possible, of course, that you'll *die* in Africa.

SHUTTLE

I've considered that.

HAROLD

Selling vacuum cleaners isn't the best preparation you could have.

SHUTTLE

I just want one true adventure before I die.

HAROLD

That can be arranged.

[PAUL appears at the mouth of the doorway. He has something amazing to announce]

PAUL

Dad?

HAROLD

Who was it?

PAUL

It's Mom.

[He steps aside. PENELOPE appears. HAROLD and SHUTTLE stand, HAROLD angrily]

LOOSELEAF

[Openly, cheerfully]

Hi, Penelope.

HAROLD

[*To* LOOSELEAF]

Shut up, you ninny!

[*To* PENELOPE]

You were never to come here again—for any reason whatsoever!

PENELOPE

I came for my clothes.

HAROLD

Sneaking in the back door.

PENELOPE

I rang. It seemed like the proper door for a servile, worthless organism to use.

HAROLD

Your clothes are at the city dump by now. Perhaps you can get a map from the Department of Sanitation.

PENELOPE

I came for Paul as well.

HAROLD

If he wants to go.

PENELOPE

You took him to the funeral, I hear.

HAROLD

He'd never seen a corpse. He's seen a dozen now.

PENELOPE

A *dozen*?

HAROLD

It's a big and busy funeral home.

PENELOPE

[*To* PAUL]

Did you like it, dear?

HAROLD

It isn't a matter of *liking*. It's a matter of getting *used* to death—as a perfectly natural thing. Would you mind leaving? No woman ever walks out on Harold Ryan, and then comes back—for anything.

PENELOPE

Unless she has nerve.

HAROLD

More nerve than the doctor, I must admit. He hasn't been home for two days. Has he suddenly lost interest in sleep and color television—and the violin?

PENELOPE

He knows you shattered his violin.

HAROLD

I'm dying to hear of his reaction. The thrill of smashing something isn't in the smashing, but in the owner's reactions.

PENELOPE

He cried.

HAROLD

About a broomstick and a cigar box—and the attenuated intestines of an alley cat.

PENELOPE

Two hundred years old.

HAROLD

He feels awful *loss*—which was precisely my intention.

PENELOPE

[Moving toward the violin, and, incidentally, placing herself much closer to SHUTTLE*]*

He had hoped that someone would be playing it still—two hundred years from now.

HAROLD

[Echoing, expressing the futility of such long-term expectations]

Hope.

[He spots the vacuum cleaner, probes it with his toe, asks SHUTTLE *with seriousness]*

Do you hope with all your heart that someone will be using this vacuum cleaner two hundred years from now?

*[*SHUTTLE *starts to answer, but stops, supposing that he is being made sport of]*

Fifty years?

SHUTTLE

You're making a joke.

HAROLD

[Not joking]

I'm interested in long-term expectations.

SHUTTLE

[Flatly, protecting his dignity]

It's engineered to last about fifteen years.

HAROLD

[Downstage center, addressing the civilized world]

Things. Oh—you silly people and your things. Things, things, things.

PENELOPE

[To SHUTTLE, as HAROLD reflects majestically on the emptiness of materialism]

You and Harold are *friends*?

SHUTTLE

[Revealing how mixed and worried his feelings are]

He's the most wonderful guy I ever met, Penelope. He's the most complicated guy I ever met. I can't believe it, but he's going to take me to Africa with him.

HAROLD

Things.

PENELOPE

You feel I've done a dreadful thing—leaving him?

SHUTTLE

[Almost hypnotized]

If *I* were married to him, *I* sure wouldn't walk out.

HAROLD

[Directly to the audience]

Never mind the condition of your body and your spirit!
Look after your things, your things!

PENELOPE

[To LOOSELEAF]

And you, Colonel? Let me guess: You don't know.

LOOSELEAF

I dunno.

HAROLD

[To the audience]

Go live in a safe-deposit box—with your things.

LOOSELEAF

Jesus—I wouldn't want to be married to *him*. You
know?

HAROLD

What's this?

LOOSELEAF

I wouldn't want to be married to *me*. We're too crazy. You know?

HAROLD

In what way, pray tell?

LOOSELEAF

I didn't like that violin thing. That was sad.

HAROLD

Tit for tat—as simple as that.

LOOSELEAF

You never *played* a violin.

HAROLD

You *did*?

LOOSELEAF

Yeah. I practically forgot. But after you busted that thing, I got to thinking, "Jesus—maybe I'll start the violin again." That was a mean, childish thing—busting that violin. That didn't just belong to Woodly. That belonged to *everybody*. Maybe he would have sold it to me, and I could have some fun. Then I could sell it to somebody else, and he could have some fun. After you busted the violin, boy, and Penelope walked out, I thought to myself, "Jesus—who could blame her?"

HAROLD

Maybe it's time *you* got out.

LOOSELEAF

Me?

HAROLD

You.

LOOSELEAF

Okay.

[Pause]

Okay.

HAROLD

You're an imbecile.

LOOSELEAF

I know you think that.

HAROLD

Everybody thinks that.

LOOSELEAF

Anybody who'd drop an atom bomb on a city has to be pretty dumb.

HAROLD

The one direct, decisive, intelligent act of your life!

LOOSELEAF

[Shaking his head]

I don't think so.

[*Pause*]

It *could* have been.

HAROLD

If what?

LOOSELEAF

If I *hadn't* done it. If I'd said to myself, "Screw it. I'm going to let all those people down there live."

HAROLD

They were enemies. We were at war.

LOOSELEAF

Yeah, Jesus—but wars would be a lot better, I think, if guys would say to themselves sometimes, "Jesus—I'm not going to do that to the enemy. That's *too* much." You could have been the manufacturer of that violin there, even though you don't know how to make a violin, just by not busting it up. I could have been the father of all those people in Nagasaki, and the mother, too, just by not dropping the bomb.

[*Pause*]

I sent 'em to Heaven instead—and I don't think there *is* one.

HAROLD

Goodbye, Looseleaf.

[*LOOSELEAF walks around and gathers his things*]

LOOSELEAF

So long, you guys.

PENELOPE

What will you do, Colonel?

LOOSELEAF

I dunno. Marry the first whore who's nice to me, I guess.
Get a job in a motorcycle shop. So long, you guys.

*[PENELOPE kisses LOOSELEAF. Everybody but HAROLD
acknowledges his departure in some way. HAROLD turns his back.
LOOSELEAF exits, closes door. Silence]*

SHUTTLE

Who's going to fly our helicopter now?

HAROLD

[Blackly, tautly]

What?

SHUTTLE

We got to get another pilot.

HAROLD

For what?

SHUTTLE

For *Africa.*

HAROLD

Do you really think that Harold Ryan would go to Africa
with a vacuum cleaner salesman?

SHUTTLE

You *invited* me.

HAROLD

To make an ass of yourself.

SHUTTLE

What went wrong?

HAROLD

We're ahead of schedule, that's all. You're finding out here what you would have found out in Africa—that you are a rabbit, born to be eaten alive.

SHUTTLE

Gee whiz—

HAROLD

It would have been fun to see you drop your rifle and run the first time an elephant charged us.

SHUTTLE

I wouldn't drop my gun.

HAROLD

You're hollow, like a woman.

SHUTTLE

I'm smarter than Looseleaf.

HAROLD

He can shoot! He can hold his ground! He can attack! You're in your proper profession right now—sucking up dirt for frumpish housewives, closet drunkards every one.

SHUTTLE

[Close to tears]

How do you *know* how I'd act in Africa?

HAROLD

Look how you're acting now! This is a moment of truth, and you're almost crying. Slug me!

SHUTTLE

You're my buddy.

HAROLD

Out! Out!

SHUTTLE

No matter what you say to me, I still think you're the greatest guy I ever knew.

HAROLD

Out!

SHUTTLE

You—you aren't going to have any *friends* left, if you don't watch out.

HAROLD

Thank God!

[He propels SHUTTLE *out the door and slams it. He faces* PENELOPE *and* PAUL, *speaks with malicious calm]*

Well—what have we here? A family.

PENELOPE

Almost a Christmas scene.

HAROLD

Goodbye, goodbye, goodbye.

PENELOPE

Just one favor.

HAROLD

Money? There's plenty of that. Mildred got the brewery. You'll probably get the baseball team.

PENELOPE

I want you to tell me that you loved me once.

[HAROLD *is about to dismiss this request majestically, but* PENELOPE *cuts him off with a sharp, dangerous warning*]

I *mean* it! I must have that, and so must Paul. Tell him that he was conceived in love, even though you hate me now. Tell both of us that somewhere in our lives was love.

[HAROLD *experiments inwardly with responses of various kinds, obviously saying them to himself, directing himself with his hands. Nothing quite satisfies him*]

HAROLD

Testimonials of that sort are—are beyond my range. I don't do them well.

[*Sincerely, not liking to fail in any area*]

That's a failing, I know.

PENELOPE

[Accepting this ruefully]

I see.

PAUL

I don't care. I don't care if there was love or not. That's all right. I'm going to go to my room and close the door. I don't want to *hear* any more.

[PAUL exits wretchedly to his room]

HAROLD

See how you've upset him. He was so merry and hale before you came home.

PENELOPE

How unhappy he's going to be—alone in his room.

HAROLD

He'll play with his rifle, I expect. That will cheer him up.

PENELOPE

Rifle?

HAROLD

I bought him a twenty-two yesterday—on the way home from Hamburger Heaven. And where is the good doctor? Have you two feathered a love nest somewhere?

PENELOPE

He's in East St. Louis with his mother—visiting an aunt.

HAROLD

Last I heard, his mother was going alone.

PENELOPE

He's *afraid* of you, Harold. He knew you'd want to fight him. He doesn't know anything about fighting. He *hates* pain.

HAROLD

And you, a supposedly healthy woman, do not detest him for his cowardice?

PENELOPE

It seems highly intelligent to me.

HAROLD

What kind of a country has this become? The men wear beads and refuse to fight—and the women *adore* them. America's days of greatness are over. It has drunk the blue soup.

PENELOPE

Blue soup?

HAROLD

An Indian narcotic we were forced to drink. It put us in a haze—a honey-colored haze which was lavender around the edge. We laughed, we sang, we snoozed. When a bird called, we answered back. Every living thing was our brother or our sister, we thought. Looseleaf stepped on a cockroach six inches long, and we cried. We had a funeral

that went on for five days—for the *cockroach*! I sang "Oh
Promise Me." Can you imagine? Where the hell did I ever
learn the words to "Oh Promise Me"? Looseleaf delivered
a lecture on maintenance procedures for the hydraulic
system of a B-36. All the time we were drinking more blue
soup, more blue soup! Never stopped drinking blue soup.
Blue soup all the time. We'd go out after food in that
honey-colored haze, and everything that was edible had a
penumbra of lavender.

PENELOPE

Sounds quite beautiful.

HAROLD

[Angered]

Beautiful, you say? It wasn't life, it wasn't death—it wasn't
anything!

[Anger still mounting]

Beautiful? Seven years gone—

[Snapping his fingers]

like that, like *that*! Seven years of silliness and random
dreams! Seven years of nothingness, when there could have
been so *much*!

PENELOPE

Like what?

HAROLD

[Becoming dangerously physical, seizing a battle-ax]

Action! Interaction! Give and take! Challenge and response!

[*He splits a coffee table with the ax*]

PAUL

[*Rushing in with his .22 rifle at a high port arms*]

Mom?

HAROLD

What's this?

[PAUL *wilts instantly, attempts to make his rifle inconspicuous, harmless, meaningless*]

What's this?

PAUL

Nothing.

HAROLD

That's a *rifle* you have?

PAUL

No.

HAROLD

Of course it is. Is it loaded?

PAUL

No.

HAROLD

Open the bolt!

[PAUL *obeys. A cartridge pops out*]

That's a cartridge, if I'm not mistaken. Gunpowder, bullet, cartridge case, and fulminate of mercury percussion cap— all set to go.

PAUL

I was cleaning it.

HAROLD

Pick up that cartridge and slip it back into the chamber— where it belongs.

PAUL

Gee whiz, Dad—

HAROLD

Welcome to manhood, you little sparrowfart! Load that gun!

PAUL

[*Bleatingly*]

Dad—

HAROLD

Too late! It's man to man now. Protecting your mother from me, are you? Protect her!

PENELOPE

He's a child!

HAROLD

With an iron penis three feet long. Load it, boy.

PENELOPE

You're begging him to *kill* you?

HAROLD

If he thinks he's man enough.

PENELOPE

[Amazed by sudden insight]

That's really what you want. You become furious when people won't make you dead.

HAROLD

I'm teaching my son to be a man.

PENELOPE

So he can kill you. You hate your own life that much. You beg for a hero to kill you.

HAROLD

I plan to live one hundred years!

PENELOPE

No you don't.

HAROLD

If that's the case—what's to prevent my killing myself?

PENELOPE

Honor, I suppose.

HAROLD

What a handsome word.

PENELOPE

[*Wonderingly*]

But it's all balled up in your head with death. The highest honor is death. When you talk of these animals, one by one, you don't just talk of killing them. You *honored* them with death. Harold—it is not honor to be killed.

HAROLD

If you've lived a good life, fought well—

PENELOPE

It's still just death, the absence of life—no honor at all. It's worse than the blue soup by far—that nothingness. To you, though, it's the honor that crowns them all.

HAROLD

May I continue with the rearing of my son?

[*To* PAUL]

Load that gun!

[PAUL *shakes his head*]

Load it!

[PAUL *refuses*]

Then *speak,* by God! Can you fight with words?

PAUL

I don't want to fight you.

HAROLD

Get mad! Tell me you don't like the way I treat your mother! Tell me you wish I'd never come home!

PAUL

[Weakly]

It's your house, Dad.

HAROLD

[Throwing up his hands]

Everybody simply *evaporates*!

[Including the audience, inviting it to share his indignation]

There are great issues to be fought out here—or to be argued, at least. The enemy, the champion of all who oppose me, is in East St. Louis with his mother and his aunt! I have so far done battle with a woman and a child and a violin.

PENELOPE

The old heroes are going to have to get used to this, Harold—the new heroes who refuse to fight. They're trying to save the planet. There's no time for battle, no point to battle anymore.

HAROLD

I feel mocked, insulted, with no sort of satisfaction in prospect. We don't have to fight with steel. I can fight with words. I'm not an inarticulate ape, you know, who grabs a rock for want of a vocabulary. Call him up in East St. Louis, Penelope. Tell him to come here.

PENELOPE

No.

HAROLD

[Emptily, turning away]

No.

[Pause. He contemplates PAUL*]*

And my son, the only son of Harold Ryan—he's going to grow up to be a vanisher, too?

PENELOPE

I don't know. I hope he never hunts. I hope he never kills another human being.

HAROLD

[To PAUL, *quietly]*

You hope this, too?

PAUL

I don't know what I hope. But I don't think you care what I hope, anyway. You don't know me.

[Indicating PENELOPE*]*

You don't know her, either. I don't think you know anybody. You talk to everybody just the same.

HAROLD

I'm talking to you *gently* now.

PAUL

Yeah. But it's going to get loud again.

PENELOPE

He's right, Harold. To you, we're simply pieces in a game—this one labeled "woman," that one labeled "son." There is no piece labeled "enemy" and you are confused.

[Lion doorbell rings. PAUL goes to answer it]

HAROLD

There won't be anybody out there. That's the new style: nobody anywhere.

[PAUL, aghast, admits NORBERT WOODLY. WOODLY is high as a kite on his own adrenaline]

PENELOPE

[Aghast, chokingly]

Get out of here.

WOODLY

It's really that bad?

[He comes farther into the room, bravely]

PENELOPE

You fool, you fool.

WOODLY

Oh—look at the poor, crucified violin, would you?

HAROLD

It died for your sins.

WOODLY

This little corpse is intended as a lesson?

HAROLD

There's a certain amount of information there.

WOODLY

Lest we forget how cruel you are.

PENELOPE

[Moving to the telephone]

I'm going to call the police.

HAROLD

[Frighteningly]

Don't!

WOODLY

I agree.

[Closes door. PENELOPE backs away from the phone, drifts toward PAUL, who still holds his rifle]

HAROLD

This is man to man.

WOODLY

It's healer to killer. Is that the same thing?

HAROLD

What brought you back?

WOODLY

The same hairy, humorless old gods who move you from hither to yon. "Honor," if you like.

HAROLD

[To PENELOPE]

He's a champion after all.

WOODLY

Of the corpses and cripples you create for our
instruction—when all we can learn from them is this: how
cruel you are.

PENELOPE

This is suicide.

[To PAUL]

Go get the police.

HAROLD

Stop!

[PAUL stops]

There's going to be no bloodshed here. I know how he'll
fight—the only way he can fight: with words. The truth.

[To WOODLY]

Am I correct?

WOODLY

Yes.

HAROLD

I can defeat him with anything from flavored toothpicks to
siege howitzers. But he got it into his little head that he

could come here and demolish Harold Ryan with words.
The *truth*! Correct?

WOODLY

Correct.

HAROLD

What an hallucination!

[He laughs]

Oh, dear, dear, dear, dear. Oh dearie me.

WOODLY

You haven't heard me yet.

HAROLD

You intend to crack my eardrums with your voice? Will I
bleed from my every orifice? Who will clean up this awful
mess?

WOODLY

We'll find out now, won't we?

PENELOPE

No, we won't. No matter how it begins, it will end in
death. Because it always does. Isn't that always how it ends,
Harold—in *death*?

HAROLD

There has to be a threat of some sort, nobility of some
sort, glamor of some sort, sport of some sort. These
elements are lacking.

WOODLY

You're a filthy, rotten bastard.

HAROLD

[Pretending to be wounded]

Oooooo. That hurt.

WOODLY

You're old—so old.

HAROLD

Now who's being cruel?

WOODLY

A living fossil! Like the cockroaches and the horseshoe crabs.

HAROLD

We *do* survive, don't we? You're going to have to apologize, of course, for calling me a bastard. That's a matter of form—not allowing you or anybody to call me a bastard. No rush about that. Just remember to apologize sometime soon.

[PENELOPE takes the rifle from PAUL]

WOODLY

You're a son of a bitch.

HAROLD

Yes—well—uh—that's another one of those statements which more or less automatically requires an apology. Whenever you feel like it. It's sort of like turning off an alarm clock that's ringing loudly. Your apology turns off the alarm.

PENELOPE

[Leveling the gun]

I'm turning off the alarm. I'm turning off everything.

HAROLD

Ah! The lady is armed.

PENELOPE

I want you to get out of here, Norbert. Harold—I want you to sit down in the chair, and not lift a finger until Norbert is gone.

HAROLD

[To WOODLY]

Whoever has the gun, you see, gets to tell everybody else exactly what to do. It's the American way.

PENELOPE

I *mean* it!

HAROLD

Then you'd better fix your bayonet, because there aren't any bullets in the gun.

PENELOPE

[To PAUL]

Where's the bullet?

[PAUL makes no move to help]

HAROLD

Help your mother find the bullet.

PENELOPE

[*To* PAUL, *pointing to the floor*]

There it is. Give it to me.

[PAUL *obeys*]

How do I load?

HAROLD

[*To* PAUL]

Load it for her.

[PAUL *shakily obeys*]

Cock it, too.

[PAUL *obeys*]

Give it to her.

[PAUL *obeys*]

PENELOPE

All right! Am I exceedingly dangerous now?

HAROLD

The National Safety Council would be appalled.

PENELOPE

Then listen to me.

[Angrily]

You're both disgusting—with your pride, your pride.

[To WOODLY*]*

I hate you for coming here—like a federal marshal in a western film. I loved you when you stayed away. But here you are now—high noon in the Superbowl! You fool, you fool.

WOODLY

Everything's going to be beautiful.

PENELOPE

You fake! You're no better than the dumbest general in the Pentagon.

[Pause]

You're not going to beat Harold. You're not going to beat anybody. You're not going to stay here, either—yammering and taunting until you're most gloriously killed. Go home!

HAROLD

She's right, Norbert—go home.

WOODLY

I haven't said all I have to say.

PENELOPE

Out!

WOODLY

I haven't told you, Harold, how comical I think you are.

HAROLD

[*Hit squarely, absolutely unable to forgive*]

Comical?

PENELOPE

[*To* HAROLD]

Sit down or I'll shoot!

[HAROLD *goes over to her, easily takes the gun away*]

HAROLD

Give me that Goddamn thing! Now get out of here, or I might kill *you*. Who knows?

PENELOPE

[*Terrified*]

You've killed *women*?

HAROLD

Seventeen of them—eleven by accident. March! Move!

[*To* PAUL]

You, too!

[PENELOPE *and* PAUL *move toward the front door*]

PENELOPE

Norbert—you come, too.

[*To* HAROLD]

Let him go, Harold. Let him go.

HAROLD

Of course he can go—if he'll just go down on his hands and knees for a moment—and promise me that he does not find me comical in the least degree.

PENELOPE

Do it, Norbert.

WOODLY

Hands and knees, you say?

HAROLD

And terror, if you don't mind.

PENELOPE

Do it!

WOODLY

[To PENELOPE, simply, decisively, unafraid]

Goodbye.

HAROLD

[Before she can protest any more]

Goodbye! Goodbye!

[He bellies and bullies PENELOPE and PAUL out the front door]

Get the police! No time to lose!

[He slams the door, turns to WOODLY]

You're in one hell of a jam. You realize that?

WOODLY

I'm high as a kite.

HAROLD

Glands. You're supposed to be happy when you die. Call me comical again.

WOODLY

You're a clown. You're a clown who *kills*—but you're a clown.

HAROLD

I love you! Have a cigar!

WOODLY

[Ignoring the cigar]

Evolution has made you a clown—with a cigar. Simple butchers like you are obsolete!

HAROLD

I'm to be left behind—in primordial ooze?

WOODLY

If you're at home in the ooze, and nowhere else.

HAROLD

This is going to become very physical. Are you prepared for that?

WOODLY

You're not such a creature of the ooze that you'd hurt an unarmed man.

HAROLD

I'm an *honorable* clown?

WOODLY

King Arthur.

HAROLD

You hope.

WOODLY

In any event, I will not beg for mercy.

HAROLD

No quarter asked.

[Taking a sword]

No quarter given.

WOODLY

Don't you laugh even *inwardly* at the heroic balderdash you spew?

HAROLD

[Offering sword]

Cut me open. Find out.

WOODLY

I've struck my blow.

HAROLD

With spittle?

WOODLY

I've poisoned you.

HAROLD

[Pointing at WOODLY *in horror]*

Lucretia Borgia?

[Looking around frantically]

Something I drank or touched?

[Understanding]

You refused a cigar. That's it! Potassium cyanide in the humidor! Treacherous lover of peace!

WOODLY

I put a poisoned thought in your head. Even now that poison is seeping into every lobe of your mind. It's saying, "Obsolete, obsolete, obsolete," and, "Clown, clown, clown."

HAROLD

Poison.

WOODLY

You have a very good mind, or I wouldn't have come back. That mind is now asking itself, cleverly and fairly, "Is Harold Ryan really a clown?" And the answer is, "Yes."

HAROLD

[Touching his forehead experimentally]

I—I really must congratulate you. Something *is* happening in there.

WOODLY

You can never take yourself seriously again! Look at all the
creatures you've protected us from! Did you shoot them on
the elevator, as they were on their way up here to eat us
alive?

HAROLD

[Blankly, as though in a dream]

No.

WOODLY

The magic root you gave me—I had it analyzed. It was
discovered by a Harvard botanist in 1893! He explored
your famous jungle for five years, armed with nothing but
kindness, a talent for languages, and a pocketknife.

HAROLD

[Blankly]

I see.

WOODLY

You aren't going to hurt me. You aren't going to hurt
anybody any more. Any violent gesture will seem ridiculous—to *yourself*!

HAROLD

[Quietly]

Don Quixote.

WOODLY

My violin is avenged!

HAROLD

Something seems to have happened to my self-respect.

WOODLY

And the hell with it. It was so tragically irrelevant, so preposterously misinformed.

HAROLD

The new hero is you.

WOODLY

I hate crowds, and I have no charisma—

HAROLD

You're too modest.

WOODLY

But the new hero will be a man of science and of peace— like me. He'll disarm you, of course. No more guns, no more guns.

HAROLD

Was I ever of use?

WOODLY

Never. For when you began to kill for the fun of it, you became the chief source of agony of mankind.

[HAROLD picks up the rifle, considers it, offers it to WOODLY]

HAROLD

Here. Finish the job.

WOODLY

I'm utterly satisfied.

HAROLD

You're making a mistake. Obsolete old carnivores like me are most dangerous when wounded. You've wounded me.

WOODLY

More clowning! Don't you see?

HAROLD

We never quit fighting until we're dead.

WOODLY

You'd be killing a friend. Don't you know how much I like you?

HAROLD

I'm going to shoot you now.

WOODLY

No!

HAROLD

My self-respect is gone—and my soldier's honor with it. It is now very easy for me to shoot an unarmed man.

WOODLY

New dignity can be yours—as a *merciful* man. You can change!

HAROLD

Like the saber-toothed tiger.

WOODLY

[Sickened]

Oh God—you're really going to kill me.

HAROLD

It won't hurt as much as the sting of a bumblebee. Heaven is very much like Paradise, they say. You'll like it there.

WOODLY

Can I beg for mercy—on my knees?

HAROLD

If you want to be found that way.

WOODLY

What is this thing that kills me?

HAROLD

Man, as man was meant to be—a vengeful ape who murders. He will soon be extinct. It's time, it's time.

WOODLY

Don't shoot.

HAROLD

I've enjoyed being man.

[He aims the rifle tentatively]

WOODLY

No.

[He goes down on his knees]

No.

HAROLD

Get up.

WOODLY

No.

HAROLD

Have it your way. We'd both be better off dead now.

[HAROLD begins to squeeze the trigger, falters, lowers the rifle]

Can't do it.

WOODLY

Thank God.

HAROLD

Crawl home.

[He turns his back on WOODLY, who stands shakily]

WOODLY

Thank you—for my life.

HAROLD

It's trash now, like mine.

WOODLY

New lives begin!

HAROLD

Somewhere in this city. Not here, not here. Tell Penelope I loved her—in my clownish way. And Paul. Tell him to be a healer, by all means.

WOODLY

What are you going to do?

HAROLD

Use the sanitary facilities, if I may.

WOODLY

Leave the rifle here.

HAROLD

I'll put it in Paul's room, where it belongs.

WOODLY

Give me your word of honor that that's all you're going to do.

HAROLD

For what it's worth now, Harold Ryan, the clown, gives his sacred word.

[HAROLD exits into corridor. WOODLY looks after him helplessly, apprehensively. Silence]

WOODLY

Harold?

[VON KONIGSWALD, MILDRED, and WANDA JUNE enter from the side stealthily. VON KONIGSWALD pantomimes that his companions

are to be quiet and to listen for something wonderful. All ghosts cup their hands to their ears]

WOODLY

Harold?

[There is a shot offstage. VON KONIGSWALD is delighted. MILDRED is sickened. WANDA JUNE is dazed. WOODLY collapses in guilt-stricken grief. HAROLD enters from the corridor, shaking his head]

HAROLD

I missed.

[VON KONIGSWALD expresses disappointment. MILDRED covers her face. WANDA JUNE sucks her thumb]

The end.

[Curtain]